Praise for Judith Hermann's *Summerhouse, Later*

"Powerful . . . Judith Hermann is extremely talented. The stories in *Summerhouse, Later* are both whimsical and melancholic, at once edgy and moving—the stuff of meaningful literature."

—*Denver Post*

"Like Kafka and Chekhov, Judith Hermann creates closely observed, carefully nuanced fictions of restlessness and insufficiency, rendering those slight twitches of feeling we might otherwise dismiss or fail even to notice, as the first shudders of the quake we spend our lives awaiting."

—John Biguenet, author of *The Torturer's Apprentice*

"A master storyteller."   —*The Independent*, London

"One of the great revelations of contemporary German literature . . . Hermann knows exactly how to choose the right details, and makes her music with them. On finishing this book, the reader is held by it still and regards the world in a different light."   —*Le Monde*, France

"A mastery of style and technique, an almost infallible sense of timing . . . a flowing cadence of narrative rising and falling . . . *Summerhouse, Later* is a work of vision, authority and humaneness—something to be savored."

—*Times Literary Supplement*, London

"In Hermann's fiction, intricately fashioned worlds reveal themselves, worlds which are utterly absorbing, sometimes heartbreaking and always starkly original. Every story here is worth reading. Exceptional."   —*Sunday Business Post*, Dublin

"An exceptional debut that gives rise to great hope."
—*Die Zeit*, Germany

"Powerful . . . [A] sophisticated and elegant book."
—*Milwaukee Journal Sentinel*

"Melancholy, muted, sometimes dramatic, but always pointed, precise and without pathos . . . The drama of Judith Hermann's stories comes from what is unsaid, from a tension between artful staging and that which really happens, but is only glimpsed."   —*Tagesspiegel*, Germany

"These are clearly tales of impressive quality and formidable originality. The feeling throughout is of considerable narrative energy controlled by a cool, calming intelligence."

—*Sunday Times*, London

Summerhouse, Later

ecco

An Imprint of HarperCollins*Publishers*

Summerhouse, Later

STORIES

JUDITH HERMANN

Translated from the German by
Margot Bettauer Dembo

First published in German in 1998 by S. Fischer Verlag as *Sommerhaus, Später*. A previous
edition of the English translation was published in 2001 in the United Kingdom by
HarperCollins Publishers. A hardcover edition of this book was published
in 2001 by Ecco Press, an Imprint of HarperCollins Publishers.

HarperCollins books may be purchased for educational, business, or sales promotional use.
For information please write: Special Markets Department, HarperCollins Publishers Inc.,
10 East 53rd Street, New York, NY 10022.

Designed by Claire Vaccaro

Library of Congress Cataloging-in-Publication Data

ISBN 0-06-000686-2
ISBN 0-06-000687-0 (pbk.)

03 04 05 06 07 BVG/RRD 10 9 8 7 6 5 4 3 2 1

FOR F.M. AND M.M.

Contents

THE RED CORAL BRACELET *1*

HURRICANE *(SOMETHING FAREWELL)* *23*

SONJA *51*

THE END OF SOMETHING *85*

BALI WOMAN *99*

HUNTER JOHNSON MUSIC *119*

CAMERA OBSCURA *147*

THIS SIDE OF THE ODER *159*

SUMMERHOUSE, LATER *185*

Acknowledgments *207*

The doctor says, I'll be alright

but I'm feeling blue

TOM WAITS

Summerhouse, Later

The Red Coral Bracelet

M Y FIRST and only visit to a therapist cost me my red coral bracelet and my lover.

The red coral bracelet came from Russia. It came from St. Petersburg, to be more precise, and it was more than one hundred years old. My great-grandmother had worn it on her left wrist; it had cost my great-grandfather his life. Is that the story I want to tell? I'm not sure. Not really sure—

My great-grandmother was beautiful. She went to Russia with my great-grandfather because my great-grandfather was building furnaces there for the Russian people. My great-grandfather rented a large apartment for my great-grandmother on Vasilevsky Ostrov, one of the islands of

St. Petersburg. The Greater and the Lesser Neva lapped at the shores of Vasilevsky Ostrov, and if my great-grandmother had stood on the tips of her toes to look out the window of her apartment on Maly Prospekt she would have seen the river and the great Kronstadt Bay. But my great-grandmother did not want to see the river or Kronstadt Bay or the beautiful tall houses on Maly Prospekt. She did not want to look out of the window at a foreign land. She drew the heavy red velvet drapes and shut the doors—the rugs swallowed all sound, and my great-grandmother sat on the sofas, the chairs, or the four-poster beds, rocking back and forth, homesick for Germany. The light in the large apartment on Maly Prospekt was dim, like the light at the bottom of the sea, and my great-grandmother may have thought that this foreign place, that St. Petersburg, that all of Russia was nothing but a deep, twilight dream from which she would soon awaken.

My great-grandfather, though, was traveling all over the country building furnaces for the Russian people. He built shaft furnaces and roasting kilns and self-dumping reverberatory furnaces and Livermore furnaces. He stayed away for a long time. He wrote letters to my great-grandmother, and whenever one of these letters arrived my great-grandmother would open the heavy red drapes just a little and read by the narrow chink of daylight:

I would like to explain to you that the Hasenclever furnace we are building here consists of muffles that are connected to each other by vertical channels and are heated by the flames of a grate-firing furnace—you remember, don't you, the retort furnace I built in the Blome Wildnis in Holstein, which you liked so much at the time? Well, in the Hasenclever furnace the ore is also loaded through an opening in the top muffle and . . .

Reading these letters made my great-grandmother very weary. She could no longer recall the retort furnace in the Blome Wildnis but she did remember the Blome Wildnis, the pastures and the flat countryside, the hay bales in the fields and the taste of cold, sweet apple cider in the summer. She let the room subside once more into its twilight and lay down wearily on one of the sofas, repeating, "Blome Wildnis, Blome Wildnis." It sounded like a children's song, like a lullaby; it sounded nice.

In those years, not only foreign businessmen and their families, but also many Russian artists and scholars lived on Vasilevsky Ostrov. Inevitably, they heard of the German woman, the beautiful pale one with the fair hair who was said to live up on Maly Prospekt, almost always by herself and in rooms as dark, soft, and cool as the sea. The artists and scholars went to see her. My great-grandmother gestured with her small weary hand, asking them to come in. She spoke little, she scarcely understood anything they said, slowly and dreamily she gazed at them from under heavy eyelids. The artists and scholars sat down on the deep, soft sofas and chairs, sinking into the heavy, dark materials; the maids brought black cinna-moned tea with huckleberry and blackberry jam. My great-grandmother warmed her cold hands on the samovar and felt much too tired to ask the artists and scholars to leave. And so they stayed. And they looked at my great-grandmother, and my great-grandmother melted into the dusk and became something melancholy, beautiful, and foreign. And since melancholy and beauty and for-eignness are essential traits of the Russian soul, the artists and scholars fell in love with my great-grandmother, and my great-grandmother let herself be loved by them.

My great-grandfather stayed away for a long time. And so my great-grandmother let herself be loved for a long time—she did it cautiously and prudently, and she made hardly any mistakes. Warming her cold hands on the samovar and her chilled soul on the ardent hearts of her lovers, she learned to distinguish—in that strange, soft language of theirs—the words "You are the most tender of all birches." She read the letters about the smelting furnaces, the Deville furnaces, and the tube furnaces in the narrow chink of daylight and burned them all in the fireplace. She allowed herself to be loved; in the evening before falling asleep she sang the song about the Blome Wildnis, sang it to herself, and when her lovers looked at her inquiringly, she smiled and said nothing.

My great-grandfather promised to come back soon, to take her back to Germany soon. But he did not come.

The first, the second, and then the third St. Petersburg winter passed, and still my great-grandfather was busy building furnaces in the Russian vastness, and still my great-grandmother was waiting for the day when she could return home to Germany. She wrote to him in the taiga. He replied that he would come back soon but that he would have to leave again one more time, just one last time—but then, then, he promised, then they could leave.

The evening of his arrival my great-grandmother was sitting in front of the mirror in her bedroom, combing her fair hair. The gifts from her lovers lay in a little jewelry box before the mirror: the brooch from Grigori, the ring from Nikita, the pearls and velvet ribbons from Alexei, the locks of hair from Jemelyan, the medallions, amulets, and silver bracelets from Mikhail and Ilya. The little jewelry box also held the red coral bracelet from Nikolai Sergeyevich. Its six hundred and seventy-five little coral beads were strung onto a silken thread, and they glowed as red as rage. My great-grandmother put the hairbrush down in her lap and closed her eyes for a long time. Then she opened her eyes again and took the red coral bracelet from the little box and fastened it around her left wrist. Her skin was very white.

That evening, for the first time in three years, she shared a meal with my great-grandfather. My great-grandfather spoke Russian and smiled at my great-grandmother. My great-grandmother folded her hands in her lap and smiled back at him. My great-grandfather talked about the steppes, about the wilderness, about the Russian "white nights"; he talked about the furnaces and called them by their German names, and my great-grandmother nodded as though she understood. My great-grandfather told her in Russian that he had to leave once more to go to Vladivostok, he was eating pelmeni with his fingers as he said it; he wiped the grease from his lips with his hands. He said that Vladivostok was his last stop; then it would be time to return to Germany. Or would she like to stay longer?

My great-grandmother did not understand what he said, but she recognized the word "Vladivostok." She placed her hands on the table, and on her white left wrist the coral bracelet glowed red as rage.

My great-grandfather stared at the coral bracelet. He put what was left of his pelmeni back on his plate, wiped his hands on the linen napkin, and gestured to the maid to leave the room. In German, he said, "What's that?"

My great-grandmother said, "A bracelet."

My great-grandfather said, "And where did you get it, if I may ask?"

Very softly and gently my great-grandmother said, "You may. I was hoping you would ask me all along. It's a present from Nikolai Sergeyevich."

My great-grandfather called the maid back and sent her to get his friend Isaak Baruw. Isaak Baruw arrived; he was hunchbacked and stooped, and he looked sleepy and confused. It was already late at night and he kept running his fingers through his uncombed hair, embarrassed. My great-grandfather and Isaak Baruw walked around the room, agitated and arguing; in vain Isaak Baruw spoke calming words, words that reminded my great-grandmother of her lovers. Exhausted, my great-grandmother sank into one of the soft easy chairs and put her cold hands on the samovar. My great-grandfather and Isaak Baruw were speaking Russian, and my great-grandmother didn't understand much more than the words "second" and "Petrovsky Park." The maid was handed a letter and sent out into the dark. At dawn my great-grandfather and Isaak Baruw left the house. My great-grandmother had fallen asleep in the soft easy chair, her small hand and wrist with the red coral bracelet hanging limply from the arm of the chair. It was as dark and still in the room as on the bottom of the sea.

Toward noon Isaak Baruw came back and, amid much bowing and scraping and many condolences, he informed my great-grandmother that my great-grandfather had died at eight o'clock that morning. On the hill in Petrovsky Park, Nikolai Sergeyevich had shot him straight through the heart.

My great-grandmother waited seven months. Then, on January 20 in the year 1905, during the first days of the revolution, she gave birth to my grandmother, packed her suitcases, and returned to Germany. The train to Berlin turned out to be the last one to leave St. Petersburg before the railroad workers went on strike and all traffic between Russia and the outside world was halted. As the doors of the train closed and the locomotive blew white steam into the winter air, the crooked, hunchbacked figure of Isaak Baruw appeared at the far end of the platform. My great-grandmother saw him coming and ordered the conductor to wait; so, at the very last second, Isaak Baruw climbed aboard the German train. He accompanied my great-grandmother on the long journey to Berlin, carrying her suitcases and hatboxes and handbags, and he did not miss a chance to assure her repeatedly of his lifelong gratitude. My great-grandmother smiled at him comfortingly but did not speak. She was wearing the red coral bracelet on her left wrist, and even then my tiny grandmother in the willow basket already bore more of a resemblance to Nikolai Sergeyevich than to my great-grandfather.

My first and only visit to a therapist cost me the red coral bracelet and my lover.

My lover was ten years older than I, and he looked like a fish. He had fish-gray eyes and fish-gray skin, and, like a dead fish, he lay on his bed all day long, cold and mute; he wasn't at all well, lying around on his bed, and when he said anything at all, it was only a single sentence: "I am not interested in myself." Is that the story I want to tell?

I don't know. I don't really know.

My lover was Isaak Baruw's great-grandson, and in his thin veins ran Russian-German blood. Isaak Baruw had remained true to my great-grandmother all his life, but it was her Pomeranian chambermaid that he married. He fathered seven children with her, and these seven children blessed him with seven grandchildren, and one of these grandchildren presented him with his only great-grandson—my lover. My lover's parents drowned in a lake during a summer storm, and my great-grandmother ordered me to go to the funeral: the last witnesses of her St. Petersburg past were being lowered into the soil of Brandenburg, and with them went the stories she herself no longer wanted to tell. And so I went to the funeral of Isaak Baruw's grandson and his wife, and my lover stood at their grave and wept three gray tears. I took his cold hand in mine, and when he went home I went with him; I thought I could console him with the St. Petersburg stories; I thought that he could then tell them to me as though they were new.

But my lover did not speak. And he didn't want to listen to anything, and he knew nothing of that winter morning in the year 1905 when my great-grandmother kept the train from leaving so that his great-grandfather could escape at the very last moment. My lover just lay on his bed and, when he said anything at all, he spoke just this one sentence: "I am not interested in myself." His room was cold and dusty and faced the cemetery, where the death bells rang constantly. If I stood on tiptoe and looked out the window, I could see the freshly dug graves, the bouquets of carnations, and the mourners. I would often sit on the floor in a corner of the room, knees drawn up to my chest, gently blowing the dust balls through the room. I thought it strange for someone not to be interested in himself. I was interested only in myself. I looked at my lover, and my lover looked at his body as if it were already dead; sometimes we would make love like enemies, and I would bite his salty mouth. I felt slender and skinny, even though I wasn't; I could act as though I were not myself. The light coming through the trees outside the window was green, a watery light, a light one sees near lakes, and fluffs of dust floated through the room like algae and seaweed.

My lover was sad. Sympathetically I asked him whether I should tell him a short Russian story and my lover replied enigmatically that the stories were over, he didn't want to hear them, and in any case, I wasn't to confuse my own story with other stories. I asked him, "And do you have a story of your own?" and my lover said no, he had none. But twice a week he went to a doctor, a therapist. He forbade me to go with him; he refused to tell me anything about the therapist, and said, "I talk about myself. That's all." And when I asked him whether he talked about the fact that he wasn't interested in himself he looked at me with contempt and said nothing.

So my lover was either silent or he repeated his one single phrase. I was silent, too, and I began to think about the therapist, my face always as dusty as the soles of my bare feet. I imagined myself sitting in the therapist's office, talking about myself. I had no idea what I should talk about. I hadn't really talked for a long time; for as long as I had been with my lover I'd hardly ever spoken to him, and he practically never talked to me, saying only this one sentence. There were times when I thought the language consisted solely and exclusively of six words: "I am not interested in myself."

I began to think a lot about the therapist. I thought only of the act of talking to him in his unfamiliar room, and that was pleasant. I was twenty years old, and I had nothing to do, and on my left wrist I wore the red coral bracelet. I knew the story of my great-grandmother; in my mind I could walk through the dark, twilight apartment on Maly Prospekt, and I had seen Nikolai Sergeyevich in my grandmother's eyes. The past and I were so tightly intertwined within me that the past sometimes seemed like my own life. The story of my great-grandmother was my own story. But where was my story without my great-grandmother? I didn't know.

The days were silent, as though under water. I sat in my lover's room, and the dust wove itself around my ankles. I sat, knees drawn to my chest, my head on my knees, and with my index finger I would draw symbols on the gray floor; I was lost in thought about I don't know what. Years, it seemed, passed this way; I was just drifting along. Could I talk about it? From time to time my great-grandmother came by and, with a bony hand, knocked on the apartment door, calling for me to come out and go home with her; her voice sounded as if it came from a great distance, penetrating the dust that had spun about the door. I made no move and did not answer her; my lover, too, just lay on his bed without moving and stared at the ceiling with dead eyes. My great-grandmother called to me, luring me with pet names from my childhood—"my heart's dearest," "little nut tree," "precious heart"—insistently and doggedly she tapped with her bony hand on the door. Only when I called out triumphantly, "You sent me to him, now you have to wait until it's over!" did she finally go.

I heard her footsteps on the stairs getting softer and softer; at the door, the dust balls disturbed by her knocking settled and gathered into a thick mass of fluff. I looked at my lover and said, "Are you sure you wouldn't like to hear the story about the red coral bracelet?"

Lying on the bed, my lover turned toward me with a tortured face. He stretched out his fish-gray hands and slowly spread his fingers, his fish-gray eyes protruding slightly from their sockets. The silence of the room quivered like the surface of a lake after you've thrown a stone in the water. I showed my lover my arm and the red coral beads on my wrist, and my lover said, "Those are members of the family Coralliidae. They form a little stem that can grow to be three feet tall, and they have a red, horny skeleton of calcium. Calcium."

My lover spoke with a lisp, awkwardly and slurring his words as though he were drunk. "They grow off the coast of Sardinia and Sicily, Tripoli, Tunis, and Algeria. There, where the sea is as blue as turquoise, very deep, you can swim and dive, and the water is warm. . . ." He turned away from me again and sighed deeply; he kicked the wall twice, then he lay still.

I said, "Listen, I want to tell you the stories! The St. Petersburg stories, the old stories. I want to tell them to you so I can leave them all behind and move on."

My lover said, "I don't want to hear them."

I said, "Then I'll tell them to your therapist," and my lover sat up, taking a deep breath so that a small stream of several fluffs of dust floated into his gaping mouth, and said, "You're not going to tell my therapist anything. Go to anyone else, but not to my therapist." He coughed and thumped his naked gray chest, and I had to laugh because my lover had never before talked so much at one stretch. He said, "You're not going to talk about me with someone that I talk to about myself, that's impossible," and I replied, "I don't want to talk about you, I want to tell the story; and my story is your story too." We were actually fighting with each other. My lover threatened to leave me; he grabbed me and pulled my hair, he bit my hand and scratched me, a wind blew through the room, the windows flew open, the death bells in the cemetery rang like crazy, and the dust balls drifted out like soap bubbles. I pushed my lover away and ripped the door open; I felt slender and skinny. As I left I could hear the dust balls sinking softly to the floor; my lover with his fish-gray eyes and his fish-gray skin stood silent next to his bed.

The therapist, whose fault it was that I lost my red coral bracelet and my lover, was sitting in a large room behind a desk. The room really was very large, almost empty except for that desk, the therapist behind it, and a little chair in front of it. A soft, sea-blue, deep-blue carpet covered the floor. As I entered, the therapist looked at me solemnly, looked me straight in the eye. I walked toward him. I had the feeling that it was taking a long time to reach the chair in front of his desk. I thought about the fact that my lover usually sat on this chair and spoke about himself—about what?—and felt a tiny sadness. I sat down. The therapist nodded at me. I nodded, too, and stared at him, waiting for it to begin, for the conversation to start, for his first question. The therapist stared back at me until I lowered my eyes, but he said nothing. He was silent. His silence reminded me of something. It was very quiet. Somewhere a clock I couldn't see was ticking: the wind wove itself around the tall house. I looked at the sea-blue, deep-blue carpet beneath my feet and pulled nervously and diffidently at the silk thread of the red coral bracelet. The therapist sighed. I raised my head, and he tapped the gleaming desktop with the needle-sharp point of his pencil. I smiled in embarrassment, and he said, "What is it that's worrying you?"

I took a breath, raised my hands, and let them drop again. I wanted to say that I wasn't interested in myself, but I thought, That's a lie, I'm interested only in myself, and is that it? That actually there is nothing? Only the weariness and the empty, silent days, a life like that of a fish under water and laughter without reason? I wanted to say that I had too many stories inside me, they burdened my life; I thought, I could just as well have stayed with my lover; I took a breath, and the therapist opened his mouth and his eyes wide, and I tugged at the silken thread of the red coral bracelet and the silk thread broke and the six hundred and seventy-five red-as-rage little coral beads burst in glittering splendor from my thin, slender wrist.

Distraught, I stared at my wrist; it was white and naked. I stared at the therapist, who was leaning back in his chair, the pencil now in front of him, parallel to the edge of the desk, his hands folded in his lap. I covered my face with my hands. I slipped off the chair onto the sea-blue, deep-blue carpet; the six hundred and seventy-five coral beads were scattered all over the room. They gleamed, more rage-red than ever, and I crawled around on the floor and gathered them up. They were lying under the desk, under the therapist's toes, and he drew his foot back a tiny bit as I touched it. It was dark under the desk, but the red coral beads glowed.

I thought of Nikolai Sergeyevich; I thought, If he hadn't given my great-grandmother the red coral beads, if he hadn't shot my great-grandfather in the heart; I thought of the hunchbacked, stooped Isaak Baruw; I thought, if he hadn't left Russia, if my great-grandmother hadn't stopped the train for him. I thought of my lover, the fish; I thought, if he hadn't been silent all the time I wouldn't now have to crawl around under a therapist's desk. I saw the therapist's pant legs, his folded hands, I could smell him. I bumped my head on the desktop. Once I had collected all the red coral beads under the desk, I crawled back into the light and across the room, picking up the coral beads with my right hand and holding them in my left. I began to cry. I was kneeling on the soft, sea-blue, deep-blue carpet, looking at the therapist; the therapist looked at me from his chair with his hands folded. My left hand was full of coral beads, but there were more still glowing and blinking all around me. I thought it would take me my entire life to pick up all these coral beads, I thought I would never get it done, not my whole life. I stood up. The therapist leaned forward, picked the pencil up off his desk, and said, "The session is over for today."

I poured the red coral beads from my left hand into my right. They made a lovely, tender sound, almost like small, gentle laughter. I raised my right hand and flung the red coral beads at the therapist. The therapist ducked. The red coral beads rained down onto his desk, and with them all of St. Petersburg, the Greater and the Lesser Neva, my great-grandmother, Isaak Baruw and Nikolai Sergeyevich, my grandmother in the willow basket and my lover, the fish, the Volga, the Luga, the Narva, the Black Sea, the Caspian Sea and the Aegean Sea, the Gulf of Finland, the Atlantic Ocean.

The waters of the earth's oceans surged in a huge green wave over the therapist's desk and ripped him out of his chair. The water rose rapidly and lifted the desk up with it. Once more the therapist's face emerged from the billows, and then it disappeared. The water roared, it broke and sang, swelling and flushing away the stories, the silence and the coral beads, flushing them back into the seaweed forests, into the shell beds, to the bottom of the sea. I took a deep breath.

I went back one last time to see how my lover was doing. He was drifting—I knew he would be—on his watery bed, his pale belly turned to the ceiling. The light was as gray as the light at the bottom of a lake; dust balls were caught in his hair, trembling softly. I said, "You know that coral turns black when it lies too long at the bottom of the sea." I said, "Was that the story I wanted to tell?" But my lover could no longer hear me.

Hurricane

(Something Farewell)

THE GAME is called Imagining a Life Like That. You can play it in the evening when you're sitting at Brenton's on the Island, smoking cigarettes and drinking rum and Coke. It helps to hold a small sleeping Island child, whose hair smells of sand, in your lap. The sky should be clear, preferably filled with stars, and it should be very hot, maybe even humid. The game is called Imagining a Life Like That; it has no rules.

"Just imagine it," Nora says. "Just imagine."

On the radio they're broadcasting hurricane reports four times a day. Kaspar says things won't get critical until the hurricane reports come every hour. Then the islanders will be asked to go to special safety zones. German citizens can have their embassy arrange for them to be flown to the United States. Kaspar is determined, saying, "I'm not leaving the Island." He is going to stay, and he expects that all of Stony Hill and Snow Hill will seek shelter at his place. The Island is in the low-pressure region of the tropical depression. Nora and Christine are sitting on the sun-dry wooden boards of the porch, raptly repeating to themselves, "Tropical depression, tropical . . ."

It is unbearably hot. Thick white clouds motionless above the Blue Mountains. The hurricane, called Bertha by the meteorologists, is building up far away over the Caribbean; it isn't moving but it seems to be gathering strength for Cuba, Costa Rica, the Island.

"Cat beats Lovey," Nora later writes to Christine, who is already back home in the city, "Cat beats Lovey, and Lovey beats Cat, dear Christine, it's not really your fault. Kaspar talks too much: I like you, I like you; he's carving wooden birds, and I wish he'd leave me alone once in a while; dearest Christine, I miss you. . . ." Christine is reading this at the kitchen table, her legs drawn up to her chest. Sand trickles from the pages of the letter. She marvels at the way things always have consequences, feels far removed from the Island, feels tired, too.

Kaspar knows that Christine kissed Cat, on her last night on the Island. They had driven down to Stony Hill in the Jeep. "Let's drive to Brenton's Place, okay?" Christine had begged, wide-eyed. Kaspar let himself be persuaded. He liked Christine's expression "Brenton's Place," to designate Brenton's store, a wooden shack in the village, the shade of a breadfruit tree; you could drink dark rum there and buy single Craven "A" cigarettes while old men played dominoes with grim concentration, and Brenton's radio gave off a long high-pitched whistle. They had driven down to Stony Hill in the Jeep, and the clouds had parted to permit a view of the high, starry sky.

Brenton had a new refrigerator. Christine duly admired it, but she was restless and kept staring hard into the darkness toward Cat's bench at the edge of the clearing— "Is he sitting there or isn't he?"

Kaspar knew very well that Cat was sitting there. Cat always sat there; all the same Kaspar said, "No idea," reveling in Christine's anxious indecision. Christine, nervous, quickly drank her dark rum, tugged at Nora's dress, ran out, and was swallowed by the darkness. Some time later, her white legs could be seen dangling down from the bamboo bench.

"Because he was clicking his cigarette lighter," she said later, proud of her powers of deduction, and Kaspar remembers the pale shadow of her face, turning toward something and melting into it. Later, when he and Nora wanted to drive home, he called her name. At first she didn't answer; then, some minutes later, she said, "Yes?" in a very sleepy and soft voice, before jumping up off the bench and silently getting into the Jeep. Kaspar knows that she kissed Cat and made him God-knows-what kind of promises; he doesn't approve.

But it's Nora and Christine's first time on the Island. Kaspar doesn't miss a chance to repeat this every day: he sings it to himself. After a week of this Nora says firmly, "Kaspar, enough now."

"You're always so amazed by every little thing," Kaspar says. " 'Look at those guavas' and 'Look at that sunset sky'—that's just as ridiculous."

In the hammock Christine yawns sleepily and says,

"Kaspar, you've simply been here too long, you *live* here, that's what makes the difference." Kaspar, triumphantly, says, "That's why I have to keep saying it—it's Nora and Christine's first time on the Island."

Kaspar is no longer amazed. Guavas, mangoes, papayas, lemons as big as a child's head. Coconuts, lianas, azaleas. Spiders hopping through the room like frogs, the tiniest salamanders, and poisonous millipedes. The fruit of the akee, which looks like an apple and tastes like an egg when fried. Mangoes are cut open and then spooned out. "Are you thirsty?" Kaspar asks graciously, getting a coconut from the garden, cracking it open, and pouring the white, milky liquid into glasses. "Good," says Nora. She makes a face as if to say "There's a first time for everything," then says, "Kaspar, stop watching me."

Christine collects everything. Coconut shells, black seashells, akee pits, palm fronds, matches, butterfly wings. "What are you going to do with that stuff?" Kaspar asks. Christine says, "Well, it's to show them. Back home." Kaspar says, "They won't be interested."

Since Nora and Christine arrived, Cat has been coming to see Kaspar almost every day. But that isn't really anything new. Cat comes around often; he is a friend of Kaspar's and he helps on the farm. But Kaspar is surprised by the persistence with which Cat—mangoes, papayas, and lemons in his backpack—now takes the steep and rocky road to Kaspar's house every morning in the blazing sun, silently puts the fruit on the kitchen table, and then goes to sit down on the porch, only to lapse into immobility. Kaspar watches Cat, who leans back in the blue porch chair, his eyes, as always, half closed, smokes a lot of hashish, clicking his lighter open and shut with his thumb, and watches Nora and Christine. They remain unresponsive, noticing nothing; besides, it's hot, and they're much too close to each other to be aware of a stranger's attention. In the mornings they drink unsweetened black coffee, smoke five Craven "A" cigarettes in a row, bum some coconuts from Kaspar, always restless to do something, then run down the field and disappear. Kaspar feels excluded and is angry. He would have liked to have more of Nora to himself; after all, that was the reason for her visit. He says "Back then." He says "Remember," he says "We" and

"We in the city back then," such funny words. Christine raises her eyebrows mockingly and Nora looks away.

"That was then, Kaspar," she says, kissing him on the cheek. She wants, perhaps, a new kind of friendship, maybe nothing at all anymore.

"Why did you come, anyway?" Kaspar asks. Nora answers casually, "Because you invited us," or, "Because I felt like seeing you. How you live here, and if you've changed."

"Have I changed?" Kaspar asks himself. "Did I come here to *change*?" He has no answer and feels hurt, deserted.

Every day Nora and Christine take the Jeep down to the harbor and then to one of the beaches. "Kaspar, want to come along?" Kaspar stays behind, as does Cat, not even asked, immobile in the blue chair. "All right then, see you later." Not the slightest note of disappointment in Nora's voice; she guides the Jeep in a serpentine line down the field to the little sandy road, Christine waving exaggeratedly. For two or three minutes you can still hear the car's engine, then there's silence.

Kaspar lies down in the hammock and looks at Cat through the mesh. Cat draws in his left leg, extends the right one, scratches his head, sits still again. He'll stay until evening, until Nora and Christine come back. He'll stay until after supper, and presumably he'll sleep here, too; that's what he did yesterday, on the old sofa in the kitchen. Cat's sleeping in Kaspar's house is new. It doesn't bother Kaspar. The islanders come, stay uninvited for a day or two, disappear again. It's the custom. Kaspar could go to Brenton's house, lie down in his bed, stay there for four days, and then go home again; Brenton wouldn't ask any questions. And Kaspar doesn't ask Cat any questions either. But he wants to know whether Cat is thinking about Christine, or about Nora. Christine?

Christine and Nora watch Cat while he eats. Cat eats everything with the same expression on his face, a stoic fork-to-mouth motion with his head slightly bent toward the plate, his left hand lying flat on the table while he holds the fork in his right. He eats everything without betraying the least emotion, and never says "This is good" or "That tastes funny." He eats because he's hungry, Christine thinks, because you eat to satisfy hunger, and that's all. She watches him, and sometimes he looks at her with half-closed eyes until she lowers her gaze. She puts rice on his plate, akee and salt fish. She likes putting food on Cat's plate.

The evenings are long, and Christine becomes restless. Nora lies in the hammock, plays the didgeridoo, blowing long, hollow, vibrating tones out into the night. She does this for hours, and won't allow herself to be distracted even by Christine, who walks back and forth on the porch, arms crossed over her chest, fidgety and bored. "Kaspar, why do you live here?"

Kaspar is on the lawn, watering the azaleas. Christine, an intent expression on her face, leans against one of the porch columns six feet away from him. Kaspar doesn't like these questions. He doesn't like Christine's restlessness, but still he says, "I guess because I'm happy here. Happier than elsewhere, I mean."

"How come?" says Christine, trying to listen to him, though she's already bored again.

"Look around you," Kaspar says, straightening up and pointing toward the jungle, towards the ocean, the fiery glow in the mountains, down in the inlet the misty, orange-colored lights of the harbor. Christine follows his glance. Kaspar remembers how, on the night of her arrival, she sat on the porch, knees drawn to her chest, and stared into the darkness for a long time, very quiet.

"Okay," she now says defiantly. "Okay, I know. But still, you must miss something. Fall, for all I know, snow and the changing seasons; you're not a native. I mean, you must miss the city, your friends, your old apartment, all that—don't you miss all that?"

"No, I don't," Kaspar says, sounding annoyed.

Christine slowly slides off the porch and walks along behind him.

"What do they talk about here, anyway, Kaspar? I wouldn't want to spend my life talking about papayas and breadfruit. About mangoes. Sex, children."

"You don't have to," Kaspar says. Christine counters, "You have to make up your mind," then turns and runs down across the field.

"Christine!" Kaspar calls after her in an attempt to be conciliatory. "The hang glider guy is coming tomorrow!" Christine, already out of sight, shouts back, "And when is that goddamn hurricane coming?"

The hang glider arrives early in the morning, but the islanders are already there. They must have started out at dawn, because when the hang glider's small red car comes crawling up the mountain, the villagers from Stony Hill and Snow Hill are already gathered on the porch, silent. "Flyman," Cat says, as always sitting in the blue chair, and starts to laugh; Christine watches him out of the corner of her eye. Nora is squatting in the shade, smoking Craven "A"s and drinking black coffee; the hang glider unfolds plastic tarps, pulls out rods, perspires, inserts metal into metal.

It is hot. The sun beats down, and there is almost no wind. Kaspar wonders how the Flyman is planning to take off up here, down the hill all the way to the harbor: he has picked the big taxi parking lot as his landing site. The Flyman puts on a helmet and climbs into a harness bundle that resembles a sleeping bag. Flying bag, Kaspar thinks. The Flyman now looks like an angry giant insect just before it emerges from its strange cocoon, and on the porch suppressed amusement is spreading.

"Flyman fly," Nora sings softly. Christine squats next to her and giggles. Eagles are ascending over the hill, and far out at sea a ship is blinking. Cat gently shoos away the flies and closes his eyes. The Flyman starts to run, the grass rustling under his flying harness bundle. The glider lifts off the ground, a murmur passes through the ranks of the spectators from Stony and Snow Hill, the eagles above the hill soar and glide. The Flyman rears up, the harness bundle flaps, the glider stays in the air for twelve feet and then, with a dull thump, drops into the reeds at the edge of the field.

Someone gets up and runs into the house. Christine says, "I'm going to take a shower"; morning turns into noon, unnoticed. The ship far out at sea changes course and heads for the harbor. Nora is standing in the kitchen, squeezing mangoes and guavas and crushing ice. Christine is singing in the shower; Cat in the blue chair lowers his head and opens his eyes. The islanders walk around to the back of the house with Kaspar to check out the new goats; a light breeze blows from the mountains. The Flyman kneels again, the glider rattles and rises. It rises three feet, then six, it shimmers blue, rises farther, glides in a straight beautiful line over the field toward the jungle, glides at an angle, rises higher and higher. Only Cat sees it disappear, a small pair of wings above the trees; a steel strut catches the sunlight, glitters briefly, then it is gone, merging with the blue of the sea; Cat sees the ship, now nearly at the entrance to the harbor, a white banana freighter that will be heading for England.

✺

"You have to learn to wait," Cat says that evening; Nora and Christine are disappointed because they didn't see the Flyman's takeoff. "For minor events, too." Christine stares at him: it is the first time Cat has ever spoken to her, and she doesn't know whether she should consider it impertinent now. She says, "What do you mean—minor events?" Cat doesn't answer, but Kaspar laughs and says, "Slow motion. Like a ship over the ocean." Christine leaves the kitchen, insulted.

The radio station has increased the number of its hurricane reports to twelve a day. In Costa Rica the first evacuation measures are being taken; the Germans down in the port are contacting their embassy to book flights to the United States. The eye of the hurricane, Kaspar says, is stationary. He buys alcohol, candles, gas, iodine and adhesive tape, canned meat and rice.

"When the hurricane's here," Christine says hesitantly, "I won't be able to fly home." Nora, who wants to stay longer anyway, says nothing.

Cat waits seventeen days. On the eighteenth day he leaps out of the blue porch chair and grabs Christine, who, paper and pen in one hand and a cigarette between her lips, is about to go inside; he holds her by the wrist.

He says, "I like you." His voice sounds rough and unused. Christine stops in her tracks, takes the cigarette from her mouth with her free hand, and stares at him: his eyelashes curve upward in an incredible sweep, the whites of his eyes are yellow from smoking hashish, his face is very close to hers. Christine shudders; he smells good.

Cat repeats, "I like you," and Christine laughs quite suddenly and says, "Yes, I know," twists her wrist out of his grasp, and runs into the house.

Kaspar says, "Cat has a wife and child."

Christine, barefoot, her knees, as so often, drawn up close to her body, is sitting next to him on the porch, scraping the remaining pulp from a mango pit. She says, "I know. Brenton told me."

Kaspar says, "And what are you doing about it now that you know?"

Christine lowers the mango pit and looks at him with irritation. "Nothing. What should I do about it? I simply know. I suppose I don't care."

Kaspar says, "His wife's name is Lovey. She isn't here. Two weeks ago she went back to her family because Cat started something with another woman."

Christine picks at the mango pit, licks her fingers, and absentmindedly gazes down toward the harbor. "Brenton says Cat would deny it."

Kaspar kicks the pit out of her hand; he expects her to be indignant, but Christine doesn't react. The pit falls into the grass. Kaspar says, "That's not the point"; he might as well be shouting into Christine's ear, he has the feeling she isn't really listening to him. "Lovey was going to come back after a week, but she isn't back yet. Cat is waiting. Whether he's lying about it or not, he's waiting, you understand? For her and for his child."

"Waiting for minor events, right," Christine says cynically, then suddenly looks straight at Kaspar with childlike surprise. "He would never go after her to get her back, right?"

"No," Kaspar says. "That isn't—usually done. He would never go to actually get her, but still he's waiting. When she comes he'll go home."

Christine fishes the pit out of the grass and feels a brief pain in her stomach. "He says he likes me."

"I know," Kaspar says, getting up. "You are what they call 'a white lady' here. It isn't about you, it's about your skin color. You should stay out of this." Christine shrugs and puts her head on her knees.

The banana freighter stays in the harbor for a week. Kaspar wonders whether the extended layover has something to do with the hurricane reports; the bananas were loaded a long time ago, but the sailors are still hanging out on the docks, scrubbing the deck, lying around in the shade, sitting mute and motionless in the bars. They look Mongolian, almost like Eskimos, their faces round and dark, their eyes slanted. Nora and Christine sit on the pier and look up at the huge white ship. In spite of the heat the sailors up on deck are wearing red coveralls with hoods they've pulled over their heads.

"They're going to Costa Rica and Cuba," Christine says. "Past America to Europe. I would love to travel on a ship like that sometime. Now. We could ask them if they'd take us along."

Nora says nothing. She looks up at the Mongolian sailors, would like to be able to see their eyes properly. Christine leans her head on Nora's shoulder and feels close to tears.

"Oh, Christine," Nora says. "This is a vacation. Visiting, get it? That's all. You pack your suitcase, and three, four weeks later you unpack it again. You arrive and stay and leave again, and what is making you sad is something entirely different. You'll be flying home soon, and we're not going to sail to Cuba and Costa Rica on that banana freighter."

"Are you coming back with me?" Christine asks, and Nora says, "No. I think I'll stay with Kaspar a little longer." Christine looks at her sideways, then says, "Why?" and narrows her eyes.

Nora shrugs. "Maybe I feel sorry for him? Maybe I owe him something because of what used to be? Maybe I think he needs some company? I don't know. I'm simply staying."

Christine repeats, "You're simply staying," then laughs, says, "Belafonte's 'Jamaica Farewell,' do you know that? 'Sad to say, I'm on my way, won't be back for many a da-ay.'"

" 'My heart is down, my head is turning around,' " Nora sings and giggles. "Cat. What about Cat?"

"I don't know," Christine says. "I come and stay and leave again. What should there be?"

That evening when Cat sits down on the porch next to Christine, Kaspar and Nora get up. Christine turns toward them, surprised, wants to say something, says nothing. They go into the house and pull the door shut behind them. Cat sits next to her, silent. Christine is silent, too. They look down across the field; in the jungle, fires are lit; there is scarcely a breeze. Christine feels Cat's hand on her head, he's tugging at the elastic holding her hair; it tweaks a bit; her braid comes loose and her hair falls down her shoulders. Cat turns a strand around his finger and smooths it, Christine gets goosebumps on her arms and neck. Cat puts his hand on the back of her neck. Christine bows her head and closes her eyes at the very gentle pressure of Cat's hand at the nape of her neck; she feels dizzy. "One night," Cat says. "No," Christine says. "That won't work." She gets up and takes back her hair elastic. Cat laughs quietly and softly hits his thigh with the flat of his hand. Nora and Kaspar are sitting in the kitchen, mute, their faces tense. "Thanks," Christine says to them. "Thanks a lot, that really wasn't necessary. Shit." She slams the door to her room behind her and bolts it.

"Lucky," Kaspar says, and Nora asks, "Who was lucky, Christine or Cat?"

Two days later Lovey comes back. She suddenly turns up at the edge of the hill and stops there; she is accompanied by two women, one holding a white parasol over her, the other carrying a child in her arms. Lovey stands there, immobile, and looks up toward the house. Cat is sitting on the blue porch chair, his eyes as usual half closed; it isn't clear whether he even sees her. Nora and Christine, on their way to the beach, stop beside the Jeep and stare at Lovey. That's her, Christine thinks, feeling strangely breathless. The second woman impassively holds the parasol over Lovey's head. Lovey stares at the house, arms crossed over her chest, and makes no attempt to come closer. Cat seems to withstand her gaze. Nora and Christine stand still and don't move. Then Cat gets up and jumps down off the porch, his face grim as he walks stiffly toward Lovey, five steps, seven, twelve, Christine is counting. Directly in front of Lovey he stops.

The white parasol sways a little. Lovey says some-thing, Cat replies. They stand facing each other. "What did she say, what did she say?" Christine whispers, and Nora hisses, "I couldn't hear!"

Cat turns and goes back to the house. Lovey turns her head and looks at Nora and Christine. "She's putting a spell on us!" Nora whispers, pinching Christine's arm; Christine feels her heart leap. Lovey grabs the parasol and closes it; the three women swing their hips and disappear as suddenly as they came.

Cat sits down in the blue chair. Christine steps onto the porch every five minutes, circles around him, waters the azaleas, clears her throat, moves chairs around, carries coconuts into the house. Cat doesn't react. He sits there like that for two hours; then he gets up and without saying a word walks to the back of the house. Christine knows he's taking the shortcut to Stony Hill, the one you can only take with a machete in your hand and rage in your belly.

The game is called Imagining a Life Like That. You can play it in the evening when you're sitting at Brenton's, on the step that leads up to his store, in the dark, with cigarettes and a glass of rum and Coke. You can play it if you have a small sleeping child in your arms, a child whose frizzy hair smells of salt. Nora imagines Brenton standing behind the worn counter. Christine chooses Cat, who, since Lovey came back, no longer sits on Kaspar's porch, but instead plays dominoes with the old men or retreats to the bamboo bench at the far edge of the clearing.

"Imagine," Nora says. "Imagine the child in your arms is your own. It is tired after a long hot day. Cat is your husband. He's playing a game of dominoes and drinking a little rum. You rock your child and wait until Cat is finished; then you walk home on the Stony Hill road. There are no street lamps, only the stars above you. Cat carries the child and walks in front; he is very strong, of course, because he works in the fields all day. You walk like that through the night into the jungle, and from time to time he has to clear the path with his machete; you're impressed by that." Nora takes a deep breath. Christine shuffles her feet and says eagerly, "Go on!"

"Well," Nora says. "Of course the two of you don't talk; what is there to say to Cat? He's the best goat butcher, the strongest worker, he has a hut in the mountains and some money under his mattress. That's a lot. You're quite happy with him, not least because the women in the village envy you for him. When you reach your hut, you put the child to bed and then you make love. In the dark, probably. Then you fall asleep, tomorrow is another day, and that you once . . . you've forgotten that."

Christine smokes, listens, and looks at Cat. He's playing dominoes, and now and then he looks up and gives her a hint of an aggressive smile. Nora rubs spit on the mosquito bites on her legs and scratches them with relish. She says, "Go on. It's your turn."

"And when all of us have gone," Christine says, "you kiss Brenton, turn off the radio, close the shutters, and it becomes quiet. You put away the glasses and the rum and count the day's take. You wonder whether the next thing you want to buy is a refrigerator or, after all this time, a very small television set. Brenton is a good man. He sells rum, cigarettes, bread, adhesive tape, paper and pencils. People say he has a lot of money under his mattress; you would know if that's true. Brenton is gentle, and has never gotten into a fight with anyone; people also say you have him under your thumb. Whatever—he loves you

44

very much, and most of all he loves your hair and the little white hollow at the base of your throat. You chase the chickens out of the hut, bring in the dogs, smoke another cigarette, and then turn out the light. I think you sleep on small cots at the back of the store; I know the child sleeps in the compartment on the right side under the counter. Brenton snuggles up against your back and puts his arms around you, you fall asleep, and everything—is all right."

Nora laughs, and Christine nudges her with her shoulder. The child in her arms is breathing quietly and moves its hands in its sleep.

The hurricane brushes Costa Rica, destroys some hotel facilities, and causes a tidal wave in which two fishermen lose their lives. Then it moves back out to sea again and comes to a halt one hundred twenty-five miles north of the Island. Christine sits at the foot of the hill and watches the horizon. The radio is still issuing hurricane reports twelve times a day. The tourists in the clubs, so the islanders say, left days ago. The embassy calls to ask whether Kaspar wants to book a flight to the United States, but he says no. He is restless, spends less time than usual working in the fields; instead he repairs the roof and the shutters, carries water and coconuts down into the cellar. The people from Stony Hill and Snow Hill come with baskets on their heads and store them in the house.

"I want it to get here," Christine says sitting at the foot of the hill, her hand shielding her eyes, the sky white and cloudless. "I want the hurricane to come, damn it."

"If it does hit, you'll shit in your pants, damn it," says Kaspar, who is standing behind her. He looks at the back of her neck; she has gotten tanned, the skin on her shoulders is peeling. "You'll be wailing and blubbering. A hurricane isn't a melodrama. A hurricane is terrible. You just want it to relieve you of having to make decisions, but not at the expense of the Island, not at my expense."

Christine turns around and looks exaggeratedly surprised. Kaspar's face is white and he is biting his lips.

"Hey," Christine says softly, furiously, "what's this all about?"

"I called the airline," Kaspar whispers in reply. "It's no problem at all for you to leave in two days, they'll be flying out until the end of this week. Only then, only after you're back home, will it start."

Christine does not answer. The grass under her naked feet is prickly and stiff. I'd like to have soles like Cat's, she thinks, soles like a hard rind, and no step I take would hurt me anymore. Nora is standing on the porch, is watching her, Christine sits there and doesn't move, and Nora turns around and walks into the house.

Of course Christine kissed Cat that last evening. Kaspar didn't want to drive to Brenton's, but Christine and Nora did, so they went. Kaspar drove the Jeep down the rocky road, the white beams of the headlights eerie in the total darkness; a huge moth smashed into the windshield, and Christine reached for Nora's hand. Down at Brenton's, the children were just coming back from a soccer game, the old men were playing dominoes, Brenton had a new refrigerator, and Cat was nowhere to be seen.

Christine, feeling restless and sad, stared nervously at all the black faces. She wanted to drink some dark rum, quickly. "Bee-uutiful refrigerator, Brenton," and Brenton laughed, was very proud, put all the Coke bottles into the freezer compartment where after six minutes they froze into fat brown lumps. "Is Cat here?" Christine asked, looking pleadingly at Kaspar. He didn't answer. Nora assumed that Cat was sitting on the bamboo bench; someone seemed to be sitting there, a shadow, not quite recognizable.

Christine drank rum, smoked one cigarette after another, and was unable to really listen to anybody. Out of the darkness, off and on, came the metallic snapping of a cigarette lighter. Christine got it only after the fourth time, then ran off toward the bamboo bench—"Cat?" Cat showed his white teeth, and Christine sat down beside him, breathless, her heart pounding. She leaned against him, said nothing.

Nora and Kaspar, outside in the clearing, in the bright glow of the lamp on the step in front of the store. Brenton busying himself with his refrigerator while the children squatted around Nora and pulled on her long smooth hair.

"Will you come again?" Cat asked. Christine instantly said, "Yes," lied effortlessly, tried, leaning against him, to figure out what he smelled like—petroleum, earth, rum, hashish? All strange. The old men slapped their dominoes down on the table, and a child secured herself a place on Nora's lap. The world was divided in two. Christine dangled her legs, then Cat took hold of her head and kissed her. She realized with amazement that his jaw popped as he did, and the "Imagining a Life Like That" game passed through her thoughts like a bright red strip of paper. She kissed Cat and thought her mouth was much too small for his; Cat popped his jaw and, as he was kissing her, he looked over toward the store with wide open eyes. When Brenton looked up he let go of her. Kaspar turned around and spoke to Brenton. Nora furtively craned her neck, and Christine knew that she was trying to see what was going on on the bamboo bench.

"When you come back, will that then be our time?" Cat asked. Christine answered, "Of course, that'll be our time," lying again. She thought of the Island, as if for the first time. Would she live in Cat's house, or where? And Lovey? And Cat's child? For four weeks or five? She kissed Cat and carefully touched the inside of his hand with a finger. The rum that was left in the glass tasted sweet and burned her throat. Confused, Christine thought that drinking rum on the Island was completely different from drinking rum back home, and she heard Kaspar calling her name. Cat held on to her, didn't close his eyes this time either, then Christine freed herself, and called back, "Yes?" in a voice that sounded strange even to her. Cat didn't say good-bye either; she jumped off the bench and took a seat in the Jeep. Kaspar stared at her reproachfully, and she turned away.

≋

The taxi that will take her to the airport is supposed to arrive at four o'clock in the morning, and up until three Christine keeps thinking that Nora will come into the room, stand there sleepy-faced—"Christine, I'll come with you after all."

But Nora doesn't come. Christine sits on the sofa, falls asleep, wakes up again, and the wind blows around the house; to open the door again now and sit on the porch one more time—in Cat's blue chair?—isn't possible anymore. Christine writes a note to Nora and stuffs it into the didgeridoo. At four o'clock the beams of the taxi's headlights finger their way up the hill; the sun will be rising above the ocean soon. Christine puts her backpack into the trunk, sits down next to the driver, and buckles her seatbelt. The driver, too tired to talk, asks only, "Airport?" Christine nods and closes her eyes.

Later Nora writes to Christine: "The hurricane passed us, the sun shines all day long now, and we've eaten up Kaspar's emergency rice. Cat misses you and says you'll be coming back soon; I say—yes."

Sonja

SONJA WAS pliable. I don't mean "pliable like a willow twig"; not in a physical sense. Sonja was pliable—mentally. It's hard to explain. Maybe it was because she fit into any projection I imposed on her: all my wishful thinking about her somehow worked; she could be a stranger, a little muse, that one woman you meet on the street just once and then remember years later with a sense of tremendous loss. She could be stupid and conventional, cynical and clever. She could be splendid and beautiful, and then there were moments when she was a little girl, pale in a brown coat and truly insignificant; I think she seemed so pliable because she really was nothing at all.

I met Sonja on the train from Hamburg to Berlin. I had been visiting Verena and was on my way home; I had spent eight days with Verena, and I was very much in love with her. Verena had cherry-red lips, and raven-black hair that I would plait into two thick and heavy braids every morning. We went for walks along the harbor, I skipped around her, shouted her name, shooed away the seagulls, thought she was wonderful. She took pictures of the dockyards, barges, and hot-dog stands, talked a lot, was constantly laughing at me, and I'd sing, "Verena, Verena," kiss her cherry-red lips, and want very much to go home and back to work, the smell of her hair on my hands.

It was May. The train was passing through the Mark Brandenburg, and the fields were very green in the long, early-evening shadows. I left my compartment to smoke a cigarette, and there, in the corridor, stood Sonja. She was smoking, her right leg pressed up against the ashtray; as I walked up to her she pulled her shoulders forward involuntarily, and something wasn't quite right about her. The situation wasn't unusual—the narrow corridor of an intercity express train somewhere between Hamburg and Berlin, two people accidentally standing next to each other because both wanted to smoke a cigarette. But Sonja was staring doggedly out of the window, tense, as though there'd been a bomb alert. She was not at all beautiful. In fact, that very first moment she was anything but beautiful, the way she stood there in jeans and a skimpy white shirt;

she had shoulder-length, straight blond hair, and her face was as unusual and as old-fashioned as one of those Madonna paintings from the fifteenth century—a narrow, almost pointed face. I looked at her out of the corner of my eye, feeling uncomfortable and annoyed because my memory of Verena's sensuousness was fading fast. I lit a cigarette and walked down the passageway, smoking; I felt the need to whisper an obscene remark in her ear. When I turned to go back into my compartment, she looked at me.

Something ironic came to mind, something like, well, she dared to look at me after all. The train rattled, and a child screamed in one of the compartments at the back of the car. Her eyes were nothing special, green maybe, not very large, and set fairly close together. I stopped thinking and just looked at her. She looked back at me, a look without a hint of eroticism or flirtation, without sweetness, but with such serious directness that I could have slapped her face. I took two steps toward her, and she smiled, just barely. Then I was back in my compartment, pulling the door shut behind me, almost out of breath.

It was already dark when the train stopped at the Zoo station. I got off, felt strangely relieved, and imagined that I could smell the city. It was warm, the platform full of people, and I took the escalator down to the subway. Although I hadn't been looking for her, I caught sight of her right away. She was three, four yards ahead of me, carrying a small red hatbox in her right hand, her back one big challenge. I clenched my teeth and ignored her. I stopped at the Press Café to buy tobacco and an evening paper, and then she was standing beside me. She said, "Should I wait."

She didn't ask, she simply said it, looking at the ground, her voice sounded not the least bit embarrassed, but firm, and a bit husky. She was very young, nineteen or twenty maybe. My uneasiness dissolved and gave way to a sense of superiority. I said, "Yes," without really knowing why, paid for the tobacco and the newspaper, and then we walked side by side to the subway. The train came, we got on; she was silent, put down her silly hatbox. Just before things became uncomfortable she asked, "Where are you coming from?" This time it was a real question.

I could have told her that I had been visiting my girlfriend in Hamburg, but for some reason I said, "I went fishing with my father."

She stared at my mouth. I wasn't sure whether she'd even been listening to me, but suddenly I knew that she had decided she wanted me. She must have seen me earlier, perhaps in Hamburg, perhaps in Berlin. She knew me even before I had become aware of her, and when I had stood next to her to smoke a cigarette, she'd hunched her shoulders forward because she had decided on her next move. She had planned this, and she knew that it would turn out like this, and now she gave me the creeps. I shouldered my backpack and said, "I have to get off here." With incredible speed she took a pencil out of her hatbox, wrote something on a piece of paper, and pressed it into my hand—"You can call me."

I didn't reply, and got off without saying good-bye. I stuffed the scrap of paper into my jacket pocket instead of throwing it away.

May was warm and sunny. I rose early, got a lot of work done in my studio, wrote innumerable letters to Verena. She seldom wrote back, but occasionally she called to tell me some story or other, and each time I took pleasure in her voice and her easygoing nature. The linden trees were in bloom in the courtyard; I played soccer with the Turkish boys and yearned for Verena, without torturing myself. When it got dark I'd go out; it was as if the whole city were slightly intoxicated. I went out drinking and dancing; there were women I liked, but then I thought of Verena and went home by myself.

Two weeks later I found Sonja's piece of paper in my jacket. In large round numerals she had written her number and underneath just her first name. I said it softly to myself—"Sonja." Then I called her. She answered the phone as though she had been sitting next to it for the last two weeks doing nothing but waiting for my call. I didn't have to identify myself; she knew immediately who I was, and we made a date to meet that same night at a café down by the water.

I hung up, with no regrets, then called Verena and shouted cheerfully into the phone that I loved her madly. She giggled and said that she was coming to Berlin in three weeks; then I began to work, whistling the refrain from "Wild Thing." At night I left, my hands in my pockets, not the slightest bit nervous.

Sonja arrived half an hour late. I was sitting at the bar and had ordered my second glass of wine when she entered the café. She was wearing an unbelievably old-fashioned red velvet dress, and I noticed with irritation that she was causing a stir. She came traipsing toward me in heels that were much too high, said, "Hello," and "I'm sorry," and for an instant I was tempted to tell her that I thought she was ridiculous, her getup, her lack of punctuality, everything about her. But then she grinned, climbed on a stool, and dug her cigarettes out of a tiny backpack, and my anger turned into amusement. I drank my wine, rolled myself a cigarette, grinned back at her, and began to talk.

I talked about my work, my parents, my love of fishing—about my friend Mick, and about America. I talked about people who rustle candy wrappers at the movies, about Francis Bacon and Jackson Pollock and Anselm Kiefer. I told her about Denmark, about the Turkish boys in the courtyard, and about the lover my mother had ten years ago, about cooking lamb and rabbit, about soccer, and about Greece. I described Chios and Athens, the breakers in Husum, and the spawning of salmon in the summer in Norway. I could have talked Sonja to death, and she wouldn't have stopped me. She simply sat there, looking at me, her head cradled in her hands, smoking a crazy number of cigarettes and drinking a single glass of wine.

She listened to me for a total of four hours. Actually I believe she didn't speak a single word that entire time. When I was finished, I paid for both of us, said good night to her, took a taxi home, and slept deeply and without dreaming for eight hours.

I forgot Sonja immediately. I prepared my show; June came, and Verena arrived in Berlin. She returned my empty bottles for their deposits, bought large quantities of groceries, filled the kitchen with bunches of lilac, and was always ready to go to bed with me. She sang in the apartment while I worked, cleaned my windows, spent hours on the phone with her friends in Hamburg, and kept running into my studio to tell me things. I combed her hair, photographed her from all angles, and began to talk about children and getting married. She was fairly tall, and on the street men would turn to look at her. She smelled wonderful, and I was serious about her.

At the end of the month my show opened. While Verena went to the train station to pick up her friends, I paced restlessly back and forth in the gallery and rehung one last picture. I was nervous. Around seven Verena came back and hustled her friends past my pictures; I left the gallery to be by myself for five minutes. I crossed to the other side of the street, and there, in a doorway, stood Sonja. To this day I don't know whether she just happened to come by accidentally or whether she had actually somehow found out about the show. She knew only my first name, and I hadn't told her anything about the gallery. She stood there looking absolutely furious, arrogantly furious in fact, and then she said, "You were going to call me. You didn't call. I'd like to know why, because I don't think that's right."

I was really taken aback at this impertinence. I became annoyed and self-conscious and said, "My girlfriend is here. I can't split myself in two. And I don't want to."

We stood face to face, staring at each other. I thought she was tactless. The corners of her mouth began to tremble, and I had the feeling that something was going completely wrong here. She said, "Can I come in anyway?" I said, "Yes," and turned around and went back to the gallery.

Twenty minutes later she came in. By then the place had filled up; she didn't attract any attention, but I saw her immediately. She came in with a tense expression on her face and a strained haughty bearing. She seemed very small and vulnerable. She was looking for me; I looked at her and then at Verena, who was standing at the bar. Sonja followed my glance and understood immediately. I wasn't afraid of a scene: there would have been no grounds for a fuss. Still, I knew anything was possible but then I also knew that nothing would happen. I kept an eye on Sonja as she walked back and forth in front of my pictures; the only thing that gave her away was the fact that she spent half an hour in front of each picture. I sat on a chair watching her, and drank a lot of wine. Now and then Verena came over and said something about being proud of me. I felt pretty good, but beneath it all I sensed a strange uneasiness which I hadn't known before. Sonja did not look at me again. After she had stood in front of the last picture for a quarter of an hour she marched resolutely toward the door and left.

In July, Verena went back to Hamburg. I never tired of her—I was sure I'd be able to spend my whole life with her—but when she was gone, the bunches of lilac wilted in the kitchen, the empty bottles started piling up again, dust whirled through the studio, and I didn't miss her. For weeks the city was submerged in a yellow light. It was incredibly hot, and I spent hours at a time lying naked on the wooden floor of my room staring at the ceiling. I wasn't uneasy, or on edge, but I was tired and found myself in a strangely emotionless state. Perhaps that was why I called Sonja again, even though, in truth, I thought the whole thing was pretty hopeless, but, God, it was the middle of summer, the Turkish women were sitting in the rear courtyard plucking geese, white feathers fluttering up to my window. I dialed Sonja's number and let it ring ten or twenty times. She wasn't home. Or anyway, she didn't answer the phone. I tried again and again, feeling an almost obsessive desire to torment her, to make her suffer. Sonja evaded me.

She evaded me for almost four months. Not until November did I receive a card from her, forwarded to me by the gallery. It was a black-and-white photograph of some Chekhovian group, and on the back was an invitation to a party.

I polished my shoes, took a long time to decide whether to wear my leather jacket or my coat, chose the leather jacket, and set out toward midnight; I was nervous because I was sure I wouldn't know anyone at the party. For a long while I wandered through the industrial part of town where Sonja lived at that time. Her house was located between a car crusher and a factory, right on the Spree: it was an old gray apartment house, and except for the brightly lit windows on the fourth floor, it was dark. I staggered up the stairs: the hall light wasn't working. I didn't know whether to laugh or be annoyed; suddenly I felt that it was all too much of an imposition. But then I reached the fourth floor. The door to the apartment stood open, someone pulled me into the entrance hall, and there was Sonja, leaning against the wall and looking slightly tipsy. She smiled at me with an absolutely triumphant expression, and for the first time I thought her beautiful. Next to her stood a small woman in a long seaweed-green dress, with an incredible abundance of red hair, and Sonja pointed at me and said, "That's him."

She had invited about fifty people, though I was sure that only a few of them were really her friends. But it was a combination of people, faces, and characters that made me feel that the old apartment house on the Spree was gradually losing its hold on reality. I don't usually have sensations like that, but sometimes—very rarely—there are parties you never forget, and Sonja's party was one of those. Candlelight came from three or four almost bare rooms; somewhere Tom Waits was singing. I wasn't the least bit drunk, and yet I felt giddy. I went to the kitchen and found myself a glass of wine, and then I wandered through Sonja's rooms and had innumerable strange conversations with innumerable strange people. Sonja seemed to be everywhere. Wherever I was, she was always standing on the other side of the room, or perhaps I was always wherever she happened to be. She had invited many of her admirers: in any case she was constantly surrounded by changing groups of young men, and usually the red-haired woman was at her side. Sonja drank vodka by the glassful and always had a cigarette in her hand; each of us would be talking with someone, but kept looking across at each other over their heads. I think we hardly spoke a word to each other. It wasn't necessary; she seemed to think it was nice that I was there, and I enjoyed moving around in her apartment and having her watch me.

At some point I saw her standing near the front door of the apartment with a very tall and weirdly ungainly man, leaning against him. I felt a soft twinge in my stomach, and then, about half an hour later, she was gone. She had simply vanished.

The light was turning gray outside the windows. I

walked through the apartment, trying to find her, but she was no longer there. The short red-haired woman came up to me, her smile just as triumphant as Sonja's had been hours ago. She said, "She's gone. She always leaves at the end." So I finished my wine, put on my jacket, and left as well. I think I was hoping she would be waiting for me downstairs, a little cold, her hands in the pockets of her winter coat, but of course she wasn't. The Spree looked steely in the morning light; I stumbled along the street; it was very cold, and I remember that I was angry.

After that I saw Sonja almost every night. I got up early again, drank two pots of tea, took ice-cold showers, started working. Around noon I slept for an hour, then had some coffee, read the newspaper, went on working. I was caught up in a high—both wild and cold at the same time—of pictures and colors; I felt I had never been so clearheaded before. Sonja got there late in the evening; sometimes she was so tired that she fell asleep at the kitchen table, but she always came, and she always looked plucky. I cooked for us, we would drink a bottle of wine together, and I would put the studio in order while she softly padded behind me in her stocking feet.

I didn't know that Sonja considered it a gift that I let her into my apartment and into my studio, that she could sit at my kitchen table amid my notes, that she could watch me developing my photos and making little sketches. In her own way she took me very seriously. She would walk into the studio with an almost religious reverence, stand in front of my pictures as respectfully as a museum visitor, then sit down at my kitchen table as though she were being granted an audience. She didn't bother me because I wasn't actually aware of any of this at the time. She didn't get on my nerves because she was much too stubborn and tough. What I didn't realize was that Sonja was in the process of becoming entangled in my life. To me, she was a small, tired person during these nights, obsessed by something, who kept me company in her own peculiar way, who sat with me, listened to me, gave me a vain feeling of importance.

Sonja never talked. Practically never. To this day I don't know anything about her family, her childhood, where she was born, her friends. I have no idea what she lived on, whether she had a paying job or whether someone kept her, whether she had professional ambitions, where she was headed and what she wanted. The one person she sometimes spoke of was the small red-haired woman I had seen at her party; otherwise she mentioned no one, certainly not men, even though I was sure there were plenty.

During those nights I was the one who talked. I talked as though to myself, and Sonja listened, and often we were silent, and that was good, too. I liked her enthusiasm for certain things, for the first snowfall—when she'd go completely overboard, like a child—for an organ concerto by Bach that she played over and over on my record player, for the Turkish coffee we drank after dinner, for riding on the subway early in the morning, at six, or for watching the scenes being acted out at night behind the brightly lit windows across the courtyard. She stole little things from my kitchen—walnuts, chalk, hand-rolled cigarettes—and kept them in the pockets of her winter coat as if they were sacred objects. Almost every evening she brought along some books that she put on my table, earnestly beseeching me to read them. I never did, and whenever she asked I refused to talk to her about it. When she fell asleep, sitting there, I would let her sleep for fifteen minutes and then wake her with the detachment of a schoolteacher. I would change my clothes and then we'd go out, Sonja clinging to my arm, fascinated by our footprints, the only ones in the freshly fallen snow in the courtyard.

We went from one late-night bar to the next, drank whiskey and vodka, and sometimes Sonja left my side, sat elsewhere at the bar, and pretended not to know me until, laughing, I called her back. Men would talk to her all the time, but she always evaded them and came back to stand next to me, a proud expression on her face. It didn't matter to me at all. I felt flattered by this odd attractiveness of hers, and watched her with something close to scientific interest. Sometimes, I think, I might have wanted to see her disappear with one of these admirers, but she would stay near me until it got light outside and we left the bar, squinting in the gray strands of morning light. I would bring her to the bus stop and wait until the bus came. She would get on, looking shaky and sad; I would wave briefly and walk on, my thoughts already back on my pictures.

Today, I think I was probably happy during those nights. I know that the past always becomes transfigured, that memory has a soothing effect. Perhaps those nights were merely cold and entertaining in a cynical way. Today, though, they seem so important to me and so lost that it grieves me.

During that time Verena was traveling, driving

through Greece, Spain, Morocco. She sent postcards of beaches with palm trees and of Arabs on camels, and sometimes she called me. If Sonja happened to be there she would get up and leave the room; she only came back once I had let her know, by making noises and moving chairs around, that the conversation was over. Verena would shout into the phone—the connection was bad most of the time, the roaring of the sea and wind, it seemed—and I could use that to cover my sudden lack of words. I didn't forget Verena. I thought of her, and sent letters and photographs to her Hamburg apartment, and was happy with her phone calls. Sonja had nothing to do with that; had someone asked me whether I was in love with her, I would have replied with surprise and certainty: no. Verena, however, thought she could sense some changes: she shouted into the phone that I didn't have anything to say to her anymore, she wanted to know how often I cheated on her with other women. I had to laugh, and she hung up.

In January a card mailed from Agadir informed me that Verena would be arriving at the end of March—"*I'm coming in the spring*," she wrote, "*and then I'll stay for a long time*." I put the card on the kitchen table and waited for Sonja to find it. I knew that, without being blatantly nosy, she habitually went through the notes and papers on my desk. That evening, standing in the doorway, I watched her. She stood at the table, looked at a photo, drew things with my chalks, rolled herself a cigarette, then noticed the postcard, the front of which showed a fireworks display. She read the card and held it in her hand; she stood still, then turned around as though she had known that I was standing there watching her.

"Yep," I said. She said nothing. She simply stared at me, and I felt something akin to fear. We went out together, and everything was wrong. I felt guilty and was furious. I had the feeling that I had to explain something to her, but I didn't know what. That night, for the first time, she slept at my place. All this time I had never kissed her, had never touched her: at night we would walk through the streets, arm in arm, and that was all. While I was in the bathroom she put on one of my shirts, and when I came back into the bedroom she was already sitting on my bed, her teeth chattering. It was incredibly cold. I lay down next to her; we lay back to back, only the cold soles of our feet actually touching. Sonja said, "Good night," her voice soft and small. I felt solicitous and, in an unreal way, moved. I was not at all aroused—nothing could have been further from my thoughts than to make love to her now—yet I felt hurt when I realized, on hearing her calm and regular breathing, that she was already asleep. I lay awake for a long time. It got warm under the covers, and I rubbed my feet against hers, gently. I still remember thinking that it would have seemed incestuous to make love to her, to touch her breasts; I asked myself how it would feel to kiss Sonja, then I fell asleep.

In the morning she was gone. On the kitchen table lay a small torn-off scrap of paper with a few words. I went back to bed and put on the shirt she had worn during the night.

And so she disappeared again. She didn't show up the next night, nor the one after that. I waited three nights; then I began to call her again. But she didn't pick up the phone, or maybe she really wasn't there. I began to roam through the city during the day. In vain, I would sit around in cafés that she had sometimes mentioned, and I would stand for hours in front of the old apartment house near the Spree; she had disappeared. There was never a light behind her windows, but her name was still on the door, and the piece of paper I sometimes placed under the door as a means of checking on her movements was moved again and again. In her own way she had given me the slip. By the time March arrived I was tired of looking for her and began to get ready for Verena.

I cleaned up my apartment and tried to blot out all traces of Sonja's visits. But, truth was, there were no traces. Three months spent with a tired, bewitched little Sonja had left nothing behind; I searched in vain and grew annoyed with myself. For the first time in ages I called my friend Mick. We went to shoot some pool and drink beer, danced with various women, and in the course of a week made our way through all the bars in the city. Now and then I would make an attempt to tell him something about Sonja; then I would break off in mid-sentence—what was there to tell, really? I didn't know.

At the end of March the last snow melted off the roofs, and the swifts returned. I gave the Turkish boys a new soccer ball and cut my hair short. I was waiting for something, but when Verena suddenly stood in front of the door one night I stopped waiting. I'd made it. At night I fell asleep next to Verena, and in the morning woke up next to her. I plaited her hair into braids and gave her an espresso machine as a present. It seemed as though she wanted to stay for quite a while, and I didn't ask how long. I worked, and she walked around the city; in the evenings we went to the movies and sat in the little cafés by the water. Verena hung her things in my closet and started working at a bar around the corner; when my phone rang she would answer it. Mick said she was just about the most beautiful thing he had ever seen, and I agreed with him. The days took on a steady rhythm of their own. I felt well, perhaps even happy, certainly very calm. The linden trees began to bloom in the courtyard, and the first summer thunderstorms gathered over the city; the weather turned hot. Only rarely did I have the feeling that someone was walking close behind me on the street; I would turn around and there'd be no one there, but the feeling of irritation remained. There were moments when I longed for something—I didn't know exactly what, a special event perhaps, some sort of sensation, a change—but this longing would disappear as suddenly as it had come.

One morning in June, Verena and I rode our bikes down to the outdoor swimming pool by the Spree. Verena paid for us both, saying she couldn't wait to be by the water, and, looking for an unoccupied spot, walked barefoot ahead of me across the lawn full of sunbathers. Triumphantly she stopped in the tiny bit of shade cast by a birch tree, spread out her towel, and sat down. Sitting right next to her was Sonja.

For an absurd moment my heart beat faster. I thought briefly that this pounding was probably that longed-for change, the skip in the rhythm. I stood still and stared from Verena to Sonja; then Sonja looked up from the book she was reading and saw me, and then she saw Verena.

I said, "Verena, I don't want to sit here," and glanced at Sonja's face, which looked oddly as though it had been torn open. She had let her hair grow, she was tanned, in a blue bathing suit, and very thin. I felt terribly sorry about all this. Verena's voice came from far away—"This is the best spot available near the pool." She didn't seem to notice anything, and I felt my head trembling. Sonja stood up very slowly, slipped like a sleepwalker into a red dress, and turned to go. Verena said something; I no longer understood the words. But I heard no note of suspicion in her voice, so I dropped my bag on the ground next to her and simply followed Sonja. I caught up with her at the exit of the swimming pool. She was walking quickly and erect and from behind she looked like a little red stick. I almost ran, then I was at her side holding her by the arm. Her skin was hot from the sun. She turned her crazily serious face toward me and said, "Do we want to see each other or don't we."

The tone of her voice was the same as it had been at the train station when she had said, "Should I wait." I felt like an idiot, completely confused, then I said, "Yes," and she said, "Well then," freed herself, and walked through the gate into the street. I watched until she disappeared; then I returned to Verena, who was lying on her back sunning herself and hadn't caught on to any of it. The grass where Sonja had been sitting was crushed; I stared at the two or three cigarette butts she had left behind and fought against the sensation of having lost control.

I didn't have to send Verena away—I wouldn't have done that in any case, I would have just met Sonja in secret. Verena left of her own accord. She claimed that she didn't want to disturb me in the current phase of my work, whatever that might mean; she packed her things, gave notice at the bar, and went back to Hamburg. I think she'd had enough of me for a while. She had wanted to make sure that I loved her, she was now reassured, and so she left. I took her to the train, feeling shattered and strangely senti-mental. I said, "Verena, some time," and she laughed and said, "Yes."

That summer was Sonja's summer. We went rowing on the lakes outside the city, and I rowed Sonja on the mirror-smooth, reed-green water until my arms hurt. In the evenings we ate at little village inns—cold cuts and beer, Sonja with red cheeks and sun-bleached hair. We went back on the train, carrying bunches of field flowers that Sonja took home with her. I worked infrequently, studied maps of the surrounding area, and wanted to go swimming in every single lake. Sonja always dragged along a backpack full of books, reading to me and reciting one poem after another. The evenings were warm, we counted our mosquito bites, and I taught her how to whistle by blowing on a blade of grass. The summer was a chain of bright, blue days; I immersed myself in it and didn't stop to wonder. We spent the nights at Sonja's apartment. From her big tall windows you could see the Spree. We didn't make love, we didn't kiss, we scarcely touched, in fact we never touched. I said, "Your bed is a ship," Sonja did not answer—as usual—but the whole summer long she had a triumphant look about her.

It was the end of July. We were sitting in the tiny, empty station in Ribbeck, waiting for a train back to the city, when Sonja opened her mouth and said, "Sooner or later you're going to marry me."

I stared at her and killed a mosquito on my wrist; the sky was reddish, and a blue mist hung over the forest; I said, "Excuse me?" and Sonja said, "Yes. Marry me. Then we'll have children and everything will be all right."

I thought she was incredibly stupid. I thought she was ridiculous and stupid, and nothing seemed more absurd than marrying Sonja and having children with her. I said, "Sonja, that's ridiculous. You of all people ought to know better. How are we supposed to do that—have children? We're not even sleeping together."

Sonja got up, lit a cigarette, kicked at a couple of pebbles, and crossed her arms. "Well, for that we'll do it. But only for that purpose. It will work, I know it."

I got up too. I felt as though I had to talk sense to a silly child. "You're out of your mind, Sonja. What's this nonsense—'Everything will be all right'? What's that supposed to mean? Everything *is* all right, and so we won't get married."

The rails began to vibrate. A high note hung suspended in the air, and in the distance a train came into view. Sonja stamped her left foot, threw away her cigarette, and stubbornly marched toward the tracks. She jumped off the station platform, stumbling in the gravel, and finally positioned herself, legs akimbo, across the rails. The train came closer, and I sat down again. Sonja, wild with rage, screamed, "Are you going to marry me, yes or no?"

I had to laugh and shouted back, "Sonja dearest! Yes! I'll marry you whenever you say!" And Sonja laughed too, the train same rushing toward us, the air smelled of metal. I said her name, very softly and scared stiff, then she jumped from the tracks back up on the platform, the train roared past, and she said, "I don't want to right now, you know. But later. Later on I'll want to."

In the fall we saw each other less often; then she went away for a while. One morning she was standing at my front door, already wearing her winter coat. She said, "Hello dear, I have to go away on a trip, but I'd like to have a cup of tea first."

I let her in and put water on to boil. She walked through my apartment and seemed restless. I asked her where she was going. She said she had to work for a month, then she would come back; as usual, she obviously didn't want to tell me anything. We drank our tea in silence, then she got to her feet, pulled me up by the hands, and threw her arms around me.

I held her tight, I couldn't properly defend myself against her earnestness. She said, "Take care of yourself." And then she left.

Everything that happened after that happened out of fear. I think I was afraid of Sonja, afraid of what had suddenly become clear to me, the possibility of spending my life with a strange little person who didn't talk, who didn't sleep with me, who mostly stared at me wide-eyed, about whom I knew hardly anything, whom I probably loved, after all.

I felt that I no longer wanted to be without Sonja. I found her unexpectedly indispensable, and I missed her. I was afraid she would never come back, and at the same time I wanted nothing so much as for her to stay away, forever.

When the month had passed, I packed a small suitcase and took a train to Hamburg. I breathlessly proposed marriage to a completely surprised Verena, and she accepted. I stayed three weeks, traveled with her to see my parents, and announced that our wedding would be in March of the coming year. Verena booked a honeymoon trip to Santa Fe, introduced me to her appalling mother, and informed me that she wouldn't take my name. I didn't care. I felt as if I were drowning, yet I was infinitely relieved. I felt I had escaped from an immense danger at the very last moment, and imagined myself saved, safe. We argued a little about where we would live. Verena wanted me to move to Hamburg, and I said as far as I was concerned everything could stay the way it was before, married or not, and then I went back to Berlin.

There was no mail in my mailbox; in the studio there was dust on the pictures, as usual, and the windows were covered with cobwebs. No news of Sonja. I had the situation under control: I had avoided the worst, and now I wanted to be generous, conciliatory. Pedaling hard, I rode my bike to her house, bounded up the stairs whistling. She was at home and opened the door absentmindedly, obviously expecting someone else; then she smiled and said, "Doing well, are you?"

We sat down in one of the large, almost bare rooms, Sonja at the desk, I on an easy chair near the window. Outside, the Spree was brown and seagulls soared over the car crusher. Sonja didn't ask me where I had been. Nor did she tell me anything about her trip. She sat at her table, erect and looking only the tiniest bit anxious, and smoked almost obsessively, one cigarette after another.

I talked casually about the weather, my plans for the winter, the new art show at the National Gallery; I felt safe. Sonja mentioned the party she planned to give again in November. I said I would like to come, and she smiled stiffly. "Will you go away with me in the spring?" she suddenly asked. I, who had waited all this time, almost brimming with anticipation of finally being able to come out with it, offered her my prepared statement, loud, clear, well articulated, and above all polite. "That won't be possible, because I'm going to marry Verena in March."

That's when she threw me out. She stood up, pointed to the door with her outstretched arm, and said, "Out."

I said, "Come on, Sonja, what's that supposed to mean?" and she repeated, "Out," without changing her expression. I started to laugh, I wasn't sure whether she was serious, and then she yelled, "Out!" in a voice I had never heard her use before. I got up uncertainly. I no longer knew what I had originally expected. I didn't want to leave, not at all; I wanted to see Sonja lose her composure, I wanted her to cry and go on screaming and maybe hit me and I don't know what else.

But Sonja sat down again, turned her back to me, and stayed like that. I shifted from one foot to the other. It was quiet, and the river was disgustingly brown. I breathed, and nothing happened, and then I left, closing the door behind me. I listened—nothing. No outburst, no suppressed sobbing. Sonja didn't ask me to come back.

I rode home, very slowly; I was—surprised. I had thought that our relationship would probably go on, would somehow go on.

Sonja didn't call, and that, at least, I had expected. It was a game, I knew the rules. I waited a week, then called her; naturally she didn't answer the phone. I wrote her a letter, then another, then a third; lots of light, foolish chatter and helpless excuses. Of course she didn't answer. I remained calm; I was familiar with this sort of thing. I thought, Give her time.

I called her regularly three times a week, allowed the
phone to ring ten times, then hung up. I worked, talked to
Verena on the phone, went out with Mick, dialed Sonja's
number the way you brush your teeth or look into the
mailbox every morning. I was amused and proud of Sonja,
proud of the tenacity with which she eluded me, but I also
thought that the time had come to stop all this. I wanted to
see her. The weather was turning cold, and the first snow
fell. I thought of the previous winter, of the nights she had
sat with me, and I wanted to have all that again.

I thought, Come on, Sonja, answer the phone. Let's
go for a walk. I'll warm your hands, and everything will be
just the way it was.

But in early December my most recent letter to Sonja was
lying in my mailbox. In confusion I looked at my own
handwriting and didn't quite know what to make of it until
I saw the stamp on the back of the envelope: "Addressee
moved, no forwarding address." I stood there in the lobby
of my apartment house, uncomprehending. It was cold,
and I was freezing. I put the letter back in the mailbox and,
lurching from side to side, rode my bicycle through the

snow along the river to the industrial district; I was pedaling slowly and carefully and refused to think of anything. In front of Sonja's house I chained the bike to a lamppost and looked up at the blind dark windows. No curtains, no light, but that didn't necessarily mean anything. The front door creaked as I pushed it open; a smell of dampness and coal dust hung in the lobby. I'd always had the impression that Sonja was the only one who lived here, and I suspected that the house was now completely empty. Nevertheless I climbed the stairs. On the third floor the railing had broken away, and the steps creaked alarmingly. I thought back to the party, the babble of voices, the music, Sonja standing next to the little red-haired woman in the seaweed-green dress. The name card next to her apartment door had been torn off. I pushed the doorbell; silence. I peeped through the keyhole into the long, white-painted, empty hallway of her apartment, and I knew that she was gone.

I'm sure the house will soon be torn down. It is February. I keep putting coal into the stove, but it doesn't get any warmer. I didn't see Sonja again, and I haven't heard from her. The bare branches of the linden trees in the courtyard tap against my window, and it's time to buy the Turkish boys a new soccer ball. I keep hoping that sometime I'll run into the little red-haired woman so I can ask her where Sonja lives and how she's doing. Sometimes, on the street, I have the feeling that someone is walking close behind me; then I turn around and there's no one there; but the sense of irritation remains.

The End of Something

S OPHIE SAYS, "That last year she just lay in bed all
the time. On the left side of the bed; the right side was
my grandfather's. My grandfather was gone, and she
would never lie on his side. Out of habit she woke early,
around six in the morning, a narrow strip of sky over the
rooftops, antennas, and chimneys, the pigeons on the gut-
ters. I don't know, though, whether she saw any of that.
She lay under heavy feather quilts, her head cradled on
three pillows, stucco roses on the ceiling and the bright
glass shade of a lamp, reddish glass. Or green. I'm not sure
anymore."

Sophie says, "Sorry," and bites her lips. She looks out
the window. The windows of the café are large, and you
can see all of Helmholtz Square. It's empty, bumpy cob-
blestones glistening in the rain. The wind whirls leaves up

into the air, and a gray dog prowls around the corner. Sophie smiles out the window. "My father would come at nine, make tea and a soft-boiled egg, slice some bread, and put it all on her bedside table, the tea on the teapot warmer; she liked its candlelight. And then she would scold and nag and accuse him, year after year after year. He would never answer her back, he'd just leave. He lived only two houses down the street, very close. In the summertime he could wave to my grandmother from his balcony, but she never waved back. She'd eat by herself, there above the morning rooftops, antennas, and chimneys; then she'd lie down again, and look into the tea light of the little warmer until it went out. She would lie there like that until the evening came, sleeping or lying there awake. It may have been that there was no longer a difference between the two, the hours flowing into one another, the light wandering through the room, no clock on the table, toward night the strip of sky over the rooftops gray-blue moving into black."

Sophie looks up at the sky over Helmholtz Square, as though to compare it. The sky over Helmholtz Square is pale and heavy with rain. Sophie turns away and looks around the café, holding the coffee cup with both hands.

She still looks cold. She squeezes her eyes shut and clears her throat, her expression reserved, distant. She says, "Then my mother would arrive, warm up my grandmother's dinner, wash her laundry, see to the stove in winter, make the bed. My grandmother would put on her sweater, stockings, slippers; with her walker she would push herself like a turtle into the living room and sink into the sofa, turn on the television. She was given one pack of cigarettes a day. Three cans of beer and three glasses of schnapps, and she always hid the three cans of beer under her butt, pretended she hadn't been given any, just wanted more beer, and said to my mother, her daughter, 'You begrudge me everything.' My mother would pull the beer cans out from beneath my grandmother without saying a word. She would look around the kitchen to find another hiding place for the schnapps bottle that my grandmother—at night? on all fours? in pain, in the morning light, with clenched teeth and groaning? or triumphant?—always found anyway."

Now Sophie laughs. A little. She laughs and looks into her coffee cup. "Just imagine it. She could no longer walk—she could only crawl and drag herself around with her walker—but she found the schnapps no matter where it was hidden. Way at the back of the closet, in the pocket of a coat hanging on the coat rack, in the oven, between the flower boxes on the balcony: she would find it and drink it all and put the empty bottle outside the apartment door. I think she saw it as some kind of game. She always won. Always."

It's getting dark outside, beginning to rain. Drizzle, maybe snow already. Somebody walks past the big window, hands in the pockets of his coat, shoulders hunched. He slows down and looks in at Sophie, but she doesn't notice. She says, "I'd like to have some wine." She says, "Okay? We'll have some wine in a little while. . . . In any case, my grandmother would then eat whatever my mother put before her; she did so sighing and continually pressing her left hand to her breast. She was fat and heavy, and her fingers were twisted with gout. My mother would sit next to her and they would watch television, and then they would smoke a cigarette together, and my grandmother would say, 'Twilight hour.' Whenever my mother got ready to leave my grandmother would burst into tears and become childish and angry and cling to her, threatening and yelling, and my mother would sit down again, but then, finally, she'd go. Sometime during the night, when it snowed on the TV screen and all the lights in the streets had gone out, my grandmother would push herself back into the bedroom with the walker. Would sit down on the edge of the bed and stare into the dark and think, I don't know about what, would lie down and then fall asleep. Day after day. In the summer she sometimes had a beer on the balcony among the geraniums, to which she would whisper conspiratorially. We washed her hair once a week; then, crouched over the tub she would giggle and say, 'It itches so much, oh, that feels good.' She wet her bed and then lay there crying and miserable until evening. But sometimes she sang and winked with her left eye and laughed about something we knew nothing about, laughed until the tears came. She never listened to music. She would lie in the stillness among the pillows on her bed, in the stillness that had once been noisy, back when her two children were still there and her husband."

Sophie looks around her. At this hour, between late afternoon and evening, the café is completely empty. Candles burn on the tables where no one is sitting, and the waitress leans against the bar, smoking a cigarette, her eyes half closed. "Is she listening to us?" Sophie whispers; she pulls her chair closer to the table and cradles her chin in both hands. The waitress doesn't move. Rain beats against the windowpanes; outside, the sound of a car engine that refuses to start. Sophie says resolutely, "In that final year, my grandmother was suspicious of the whole world. She saw men in the corner behind the stove, and she would hide her purse under the mattress, in the bedside table, in a pillowcase. 'Give back what you took from me!' she would scream while my mother was warming up her food in the kitchen, and then she would list all the things my father was supposedly taking out of the apartment every morning—furs and silverware and jewelry and the medals of the grandfathers, money and bankbooks, pots and jars. She would tug at my mother's jacket and say, 'Stolen jacket.' She would gasp and call for the police, and my mother would just stand there, looking at her without saying a word. And my grandmother would push herself into the kitchen with her walker, check the cabinets and drawers, burst into tears, and say, 'I can't go on like this anymore.' Still, she lay in bed all day and waited.

"You know," Sophie said, "it's not easy. To dredge up these memories, bit by bit. I forget so quickly. Especially faces, I always forget faces—immediately, really—and I can no longer remember the face of my grandmother either. She was always cold. And under her feather quilts she wore wool cardigans, scarves, heavy stockings. In spite of that she'd say, 'I want fresh air.' Even in winter all the windows in the bedroom had to be open. But in the living room little space heaters stood around the sofa, blowing hot air into her face, and she would say, 'I don't know, I'm still cold.' Her hair was white. She would let the egg yolk ooze over her bread in the morning and drink her tea black, without sugar. There was a phone in the living room and another in the bedroom, and sometimes her son would call from the luminous distance of his suburban villa to inquire about her health and his sister. My grandmother, lying in her urine and in pain, would take a deep breath, hold the phone close to her ear, her eyes lighting up, and say into the room, 'Fine, everything is just fine.' "

Sophie gets up, much too quickly, and walks over to the restroom. She is so thin, her legs like little sticks in their heavy wool stockings. She walks very erect, shoulders held high, stiff-backed. The waitress watches her and yawns, bored; the coffee machine rumbles. No one left in the room, the rain is now a cloudburst, and the candle on the table is drowning in melted wax. Sophie comes back, sits down again, lights a cigarette, inhales deeply, watches the smoke. She looks tired. She says, "My grandmother used to smoke these long cigarettes, long, light ladies' cigarettes. She never inhaled, and she always followed the smoke with her eyes. Like me. Or, me like her. She'd knock on the wall with her fist whenever my mother was too slow for her. Once she sat up in bed, pointed at the back of her head, where her white hair had become curled, and said, 'That means that I will die soon.' Or sometimes, and then always with her eyes turned to the sky above the rooftops, above the antennas, 'God doesn't want me.' She couldn't tell more than two stories, or maybe we only wanted to hear those two. The war story—the Russians already on the outskirts of Berlin and my grandmother on the train fleeing with her children; the train stopping suddenly, no station, no town or village, and her six-year-old son needing to pee, 'Really had to pee,' my grandmother would say, as though uninvolved. So she let him get off, into the open field: the rape was already in bloom and it was a warm day. My grandmother waited by the door of the train, and her six-year-old son ran into the yellow rape, yelling childish things, and peed; just then the train started up again, unexpectedly, much too quickly, and the child was left in the rape field, open-mouthed, supposedly wearing a blue sailor suit. I don't know the end of the story. At any rate, he didn't die. The postwar story—the two-room apartment in the summertime, her husband already gone, and geraniums on the balcony, my grandmother, as usual, in the kitchen, her daughter and her son in the living room, the daughter and the son shooting pebbles with slingshots. My grandmother was peeling potatoes, slicing cabbage. 'Bet I can shoot your eye out,' her daughter, my mother, said to the son in the living room. 'Bet you can't,' said the son, and the daughter, his sister, took aim, shot and hit her target. The daughter screamed. The son didn't, and the daughter, my mother, stood in the kitchen doorway, covered her face with her hands and whispered, 'I hit his eye, the left one,' kept whispering it over and over again. My grandmother got up, potato peels and cabbage slicer falling to the floor, and ran into the living room. There was her son, the pebble stuck in the middle of his left eye, stuck there like a stone eye. 'So I pulled it out,' my grandmother would say, very simply. Her son got glass eyes, five little brown glass eyes to wear in turn, and when the brother and sister quarreled, my mother would toss the glass eyes around the room and say, 'Go find them, cripple,' and my grandmother would giggle. Why. There were no other stories."

Sophie looks surprised. Not sad, not yet. She rubs her

eyes with both hands, and presses her thumbs to her lids. There's a trace of a smile, just barely. She looks at the waitress, who slowly pushes herself away from the bar and sidles over to the table, like a sleepwalker. The waitress wipes her hands on her apron, says nothing. In a strange voice, Sophie says, "I would like a glass of dry red wine," and the waitress slinks back to the bar; did she get that? "We'll see," Sophie says. "My grandmother left her apartment one more time, one last time, when her granddaughter—not me, the other one—had her eighteenth birthday and her son rented the Lake Terraces and hired an organ grinder and ordered a huge buffet. 'A little bit of everything,' the son said into the telephone, and my grandmother lay in her bed and looked at the sky above the rooftops, the antennas, and said, 'Yes, I'd like to come.' 'You'll need a present,' my mother said. 'She's going to be eighteen, you have to give her something. Give me some money and I'll buy it for you.' But my grandmother casually waved her away with her left hand, saying she already had a present, not to worry. 'Where did you get it?' my mother asked. 'There's no way you can buy anything, you can't even leave the apartment.' My grandmother refused to answer her. Counted the days. Had her hair washed, the blue dress taken out of the closet, her good dress, she said, 'as blue as my eyes.' She stopped nagging. Looked at my father in the morning without a word, threw money at him from her bed, bills that came from inside the slits in the mattress, the pillowcases, said, 'Take it, I don't want it anymore.' On her granddaughter's birthday she left her apartment in a wheelchair, was carried out and loaded into a van by three men; while they perspired my grandmother sat in the wheelchair like a queen, holding a basket in her lap with the wrapped present inside. 'What is it?' She shook her head, almost indulgently, said, 'Oh, just wait and see.' We followed the van in our car, and I could see her, could see her white head pressed against the window: from time to time she wiped the fogged-up pane with her hand. The entire journey she looked out of the window—what did she see? I can't tell. At the Lake Terraces they wheeled her to the head of the table, between her son and her granddaughter. Everyone was very cheerful and talked to her and put plates full of food and glasses of wine in front of her, but she drank nothing, ate nothing. She handed the present to her granddaughter, who was sitting next to her with a dutiful, reverent expression on her face; it grew quiet at the table, the son laughed—the grandmother is giving her granddaughter a gift. The granddaughter carefully tore open the wrapping paper, felt the present, then hesitated, pulled the paper off completely and held up a yellow pot lid, already somewhat dented at the rim. 'What is it?' she asked—a puzzle, a symbol? She was eighteen years old and she smiled at my grandmother. 'It's the cover of the pot you stole from me,' said my grandmother, 'just like you stole everything else from me.' And then, very slowly, she raised her hand and put it over her left eye and turned to her son and looked at him with her right eye, which really was as blue as her good dress."

The waitress puts the wine on the table and stares at Sophie, Sophie does not return her look. She says thanks, and takes a hefty swig of the wine, then wipes her mouth with the back of her hand. The door opens and the wind blows in, the smell of rain, two, three customers in wet coats, their faces flushed. Sophie doesn't turn around. She is no longer cold; she has red cheeks now, and the tiredness around her eyes is gone. "I'm almost finished. The story is almost over, finished, it won't take much longer, is that okay? Later that night, they pushed her in the wheelchair down to the lake one last time. She sat there and stared into the darkness, on the other shore, little lights and the soft

lapping of the waves. 'What's the point?' said my grandmother, and they brought her back home in the van. She
let them put her to bed and turned away and said to my
mother, who was standing by the door, 'Good night.' The
next morning my father came over, made tea and a soft-
boiled egg, sliced bread, and put it all in front of her, the
tea on the little warmer, the egg yolk already on the bread.
'The tea light,' said my grandmother, 'the tea light,' that
was all. 'But it's already lit,' said my father, 'look, it's
burning.' And my grandmother said, 'Yes,' and closed
her eyes. My father left. Went shopping, then back home.
He heard the telephone ringing while he was still out on
the stairs, ringing incessantly. My father unlocked the
apartment door, dropped his shopping bags, grabbed the
phone, and said hello, heard no answer. He listened some
more, wanted to hang up again, but then he did hear something after all, from very far away, really far away.
Crying? Or screaming? A cry of pain? Actually it was a
rustling, a crackling, something completely unreal; how he
suddenly knew, I don't know. He dropped the phone and
dashed out of the apartment, down the stairs, and out into
the street. It was February, just like today, and cold. My father ran fast. Two houses away. He ran. Pushed open the

front door, ran up the three flights of stairs, he was probably trembling and afraid as well; the apartment door was stuck, I think, he must have dropped the key three or four times. He pushed against the door until it opened. The entry hall was small, and something smelled. The door to the bedroom was ajar and behind it, a bright glow. I no longer know whether it was four steps or five to the bedroom; my father stood in the doorway and saw my grandmother. She was on fire. She had gotten out of bed, somehow, and was standing in the middle of the room, next to the bed. The bed was burning, my grandmother's nightgown was burning, her stockings, her scarf, her hair, her face and her blue eyes; she was ablaze and no longer screaming, the sky above the rooftops, the antennas, gray and smoky. . . . She was, my father said later—he couldn't really say—but she was actually dancing as she burned," says Sophie, not crying, with an embarrassed smile.

Bali Woman

THERE ARE times when winter reminds me of something. A mood I was once in, a desire I once felt? I
don't exactly know. It is cold. The air smells of smoke. Of
snow. I turn around and listen for something I can't hear.
There's a word on the tip of my tongue, I can't say it. A
kind of restlessness, you know? You *do* know. But, as you
would say, what is nameless should remain nameless.

In any case, that night you didn't want to come along,
Christiane danced for me. She turned on the radio and
danced to "I've Never Known a Girl Like You," cheerleader face, red hair loose. She was laughing, and she
looked very beautiful. Markus Werner was wearing his
grandmother's fur coat and a pair of household gloves
made of pink rubber; the fur was mangy. "You're so silly,"
Christiane said. Markus Werner laid out the cocaine in

short lines on his pocket mirror without looking at her. I wasn't tired. I sat on the sofa, leaning against him; his fur coat was wet with snow and smelled funny. I watched Christiane as she filled in the outlines of her mouth with a plum-colored lipstick: her mouth was big and the lipstick was pointed, like a pen. Markus Werner looked up from his pocket mirror and stared into space.

Where were you? I had called you—you were sitting in front of your TV and said that you'd taken the wrong drugs: you sounded tired and irritable, and you didn't want to come along. I said, "Christiane has fallen in love." You said, "What else is new?" Then we were silent. I could hear the small voices coming out of your television, sounds of war, an air-raid siren; I knew it was cold in your room, frost flowers on the windows. You hung up.

The voice of Edwyn Collins sounded rough as ever. I smoked three cigarettes, one after the other. "Who is it this time?" Markus Werner asked casually, his rubber gloves making a sticky sound. "Oh, shut up," said Christiane as she looked at herself sideways in the large mirror, one hand on her hip, gazing up from under her lashes; there were small blue shadows under her eyes, and she looked terrific. "We're going to have fun," she said, and kissed me on the mouth. I clutched Markus Werner's arm and whispered in his ear—it didn't look as if Christiane was going to stop me—"He's an important director. *Very* important, you know. He's married. We're going to his opening night party, there'll be food, vodka, and everything, hey, it'll be fun." Christiane laughed and pulled me away from him.

Outside it was very cold. I thought of you in your room, sitting in your armchair in front of the TV. I knew you wouldn't be watching any old film but would be sitting there in the semidarkness, staring straight ahead; I wasn't disappointed, not hurt, just a little sad maybe. It was extremely cold. The air smelled of snow, and in the empty street our voices made such a weirdly hollow sound that we stopped talking altogether; the light from the street lamps seemed frozen in place. Christiane fell in her high-heeled shoes, and I looked at Markus Werner; we didn't help her get up. At the intersection we hailed a cab. "The theater," Christiane said. She sat next to the driver, rolled down the window, and turned on the radio. The driver made a face but didn't say anything.

Red flags were flying outside the theater, and the doors were open. Markus Werner leaned forward and said, "Hey, about the play they did here tonight . . . ?" and

Christiane gently waved his question aside. "But what are you going to talk to him about if not the play?" said Markus Werner, giggling. Christiane drew his face close to hers and said very clearly, "I don't want to *talk* at all. Understand?"

At the door I turned around once more. For one final moment I considered going back, going to your place, and sitting down next to you in front of your TV. I would have turned it off and looked at you: it could have been so easy. I just couldn't make up my mind; then I took a deep breath and ran after Christiane and Markus Werner.

In the theater's Star Lounge, long tables were set up. The food looked fabulous and there were coolers full of vodka and small chilled glasses; they had engaged a Russian brass band and switched on red lights. "Now," Christiane said, and disappeared. I got some bread and fish from the buffet, and Markus Werner stuffed vodka bottles and glasses into his coat pockets. He was still wearing those pink rubber gloves, but no one paid any attention to him. We sat down on the stairs and ate. I drank the vodka in great gulps and began to feel warm, while Markus Werner sat there, fidgeting and constantly wiping his nose. I said, "You do too much coke," and he said, "Where is he, that great director?" The director was standing at the bar. He was tall and fat and seedy-looking, smoking a cigar and drinking whiskey; he had that scruffy older-man sexiness that Christiane could never resist, and he was famous. I pointed at him and said, "That's him," and Markus Werner began to laugh hysterically and said, "Of course." I looked at the director and thought of the countless directors and playwrights and actors and stage designers who had sat at mine and Christiane's kitchen table, had used our shower, had slept in our beds; I thought of their voices on our answering machine, their nighttime banging on our door, the smashed glasses and unread letters; I thought that there was always something that wasn't quite enough, and this time, too, something wouldn't be enough; I thought of you, of the frost flowers, of the smell of smoke; I thought, We're not enough, either.

Christiane appeared. She must have been standing in front of a ladies' room mirror again, because she had twisted her hair into a knot which I knew she was going to undo at some point by simply pulling out one single hairpin, allowing the hair to cascade over her shoulders in a wave that would make me feel weary. She made her entrance at the far side of the Star Lounge, wandering back and forth among the pillars for a while, approaching the bar then walking away again, lighting a cigarette and gazing around her from beneath lowered eyelids. The band was playing Ween's "Buenas Tardes, Amigos." Markus Werner wiped his nose on his rubber gloves, then wiped the gloves on his fur coat, saying, "A real song of betrayal." Christiane bobbed her head a little, buckled at the hip, swayed for an instant, then pushed her way onto the empty dance floor, to the dead center, positioning herself on the big star, where the chandelier flooded her with red light. All this time the director had been staring vacantly at the dance floor, but now he turned away. When he turned back a little later, right away actually, he looked at Christiane. And Christiane danced, cheerleader face, hands on her hips; threw her head back and seemed to be laughing; the slit in her dress reached all the way up to her butt. Markus Werner giggled nonstop, whether because of the coke or Christiane's dancing, I didn't know. I had to laugh, and said, "Hey, she knows how to do it. She really knows how."

She danced for a long time. At some point she raised her hand to her head and released the knot and her hair flooded down her back. Markus Werner buried his head between his knees and said, "I can't stand it." The director was one blurry, fat little heap of greed. I withdrew. I drank vodka and stared up into the lights of the chandelier, feeling a little dizzy, and I thought of all the nights we had gotten drunk together, you and I, at the wooden tables of some bar or other, it was always in the winter, always snowy outside, and it never grew light. I don't remember the summers. Why not? I'd tried to understand why it's over between us, and I realized there was nothing to understand. I thought of you, of your room, the blue light from the TV, the half-smoked cigarette in your left hand. I thought that you had known all this long before I did; you could have said something, something, anything.

Markus Werner nudged me and said, "Look at that, will you; hey, what's with you? You gotta see this," and I looked over at the dance floor. Christiane was still dancing, and another woman was now dancing with her. The woman was small and slender; she looked like a child, a precocious child, her skin dark and her hair black. She wore a red dress, and when she spun in a circle you could see her naked buttocks and her pubic hair. She kept spinning, her small hands fluttering around her like birds. She was dancing barefoot, and her way of dancing was completely different from Christiane's. Christiane lost her rhythm. She tried to use her cheerleader face, her swinging hips, the carefully calculated rhythmic movement of her legs, her coolness to counter the other woman's gentle movements, but it didn't work. She saw too much. The small woman had closed her eyes and seemed to be in another world, her black hair covering her face. Markus Werner stared open-mouthed; lit a cigarette, like someone who needed one to concentrate, then turned abruptly toward me and asked matter-of-factly, "Who's that?" And I said, "That's his wife. The director's wife. She's from Bali. They got married in Bali."

You would have liked her, this small woman. She was untouchable, in a way that you always liked; she was remote, and one could watch her and think up stories about her. She looked vulnerable and beautiful, with tiny, tiny feet, and on these marble tiles, in this lounge under the light of the chandelier, she felt so unreal. Christiane left the dance floor and went to the bar. The director came over and stood next to her, not looking at his wife but at Christiane, who ordered a large glass of whiskey. The small woman kept on dancing, and I knew that the stone floor under her feet was very cold. Markus Werner looked at me and said, "Feel like talking?" "No," I said. He got up and left. I continued drinking by myself. It was getting very late. I could see the snow through the large windows—thick, gently falling flakes. At some point Markus Werner was staggering around between the columns, fairly drunk and holding—heaven knows where he got it—a megaphone; he kept shouting into the megaphone, always the same thing, but I couldn't understand a single word. I leaned my head against the banister and watched him. It occurred to me that I had never actually seen him during the day, and I wondered whether I wanted to know anything about him other than the fact that he wore this fur coat in the winter and orange garbage-man jackets in the summer. Three times a week he went out with Christiane and me. I liked him; had I ever mentioned him to anybody, I would actually have called him a friend. Did I take him seriously? Did he take me seriously, did he want something when he said he wanted to have a conversation with me—about what, I wonder? I remembered that he had said once, in a very childlike manner, "I could shoot a film about us." I had said, "What kind of film?" He answered, "A film about the fact that nothing's happening, nothing's going on between us and around us, just a night like this with you and me and Christiane," and I had laughed rather disparagingly. I watched him now—he was much too young, high on coke and drunk, bellowing into his megaphone until his neck swelled. People were avoiding him. I felt sorry for him, and thought that I never, ever wanted to see him again. I repressed the impulse to get up, walk over, take away the megaphone, and kiss him. A girl was crouched on the star in the middle of the dance floor; she kept banging her head on the floor, her forehead was bloody, she was crying and talking crazy. The buffet was bare. On the big red sofa an actress was screwing a stagehand; the stagehand was sweating and the actress was desperately tearing at the back of his T-shirt, which had a picture of Mike Tyson biting Evander Holyfield's ear. The small woman was gone, the director was gone, Christiane was gone. It was still snowing, and somebody was throwing glasses against the wall; the two cripples who rolled in wheelchairs across the dance floor and disappeared behind the columns felt unreal. The actress pulled down her skirt, staggered up onto the small stage, and said, "For baby," into an overmodulating microphone; she said, "For baby, for baby," then she collapsed. I closed my eyes. I heard Markus Werner yelling, but I still couldn't understand what he was saying. I fell asleep. I woke up again because Christiane was standing before me and pulling at my arm; she still looked as she had hours ago, in the apartment, on the street, in the taxi; she looked so wintry, so cool, so cold, her mouth frosty and thin-lipped. She shook me and said, "Get up. We've got to go, we're going someplace else, where's Werner and what are you doing here anyway?" She didn't say this quickly and agitatedly but very quietly and precisely. I got up and clung to her, looking into her eyes: her eyes were ice blue. I said, "Christiane. How are things?" and she looked at me and said, "Shitty. Things are shitty. But we'll go anyway."

Are you jealous? Just a tiny bit? A little curious and nervous, wondering where? Where are they going now? You would have gone home. No, you're not jealous, you never were. We went to look for Markus Werner and found him in the bathroom, standing in front of the sink, rinsing something off his rubber gloves, and from one of the cubicles came a girl's whiny voice, saying, "What's wrong, why are you stopping now? I don't understand." Christiane grimaced in disgust and kicked the cubicle door shut with her left foot, and Markus Werner turned around and said, much too softly, "Does it have to be like this?" "She's waiting," Christiane said. "She's waiting, and we have to go now, right this minute." Markus Werner suddenly looked helpless, as though it were all too much for him and said pleadingly, "Who's waiting? Who's waiting?" Christiane, already out in the hall, turned around, annoyed, and shouted, "The Bali woman. The Bali woman is waiting."

The clock outside the theater had stopped at eleven. The snow had formed a deep layer on the street, on the cars, on the street lamps, and the world was silent and roaring in my ears. The Bali woman, still barefoot and coatless in her red dress, was standing there next to a taxi, holding the door open for us. As Christiane pushed Markus Werner into the taxi, his megaphone fell into the snow; then she pushed me in after him and got in herself. Markus Werner whispered, "Your eyes break my heart, little sister." I didn't know whose eyes he meant, and wondered whether this was the sentence he'd been yelling through the megaphone all night. The Bali woman sat down on the seat next to the driver and turned around and smiled at us. I smiled back. As the taxi drove off, I leaned over to Christiane and said softly, "So where to? Where are we going now?" and Christiane, looking out the window, said, "To his place. Or hers. We're going to her apartment; he's already there, she wants us to come with her." I said, "Why?" and Christiane shrugged. I asked, "Why do *you* want to?" and she said, "It doesn't really matter."

The key to your apartment is on the ledge above the door. I know that. I could stand on tiptoe in the dark hallway, feel for it with my fingers and take it down, put it into the keyhole, quietly unlock the door. I could walk across the hall to your room: you would've turned off the television set by now and gone to sleep. I could stand next to your bed, watch you while you sleep, lie down next to you; you wouldn't notice a thing. But the key isn't there for me. I know that. It's lying there for the one person we've never talked about, it's there, ready for her. When the time comes she'll get up on her toes, feel around for it, unlock the door, put her suitcases next to your bed, and wake you. That's how it is, isn't it? You're waiting. You don't know her, this person, but you know she'll come, and that's what you're waiting for, sitting there and looking at the frost flowers and waiting. I am waiting, too.

In any case, the Bali woman had no key. She didn't

have a key to her own apartment, or she pretended not to have one. We stood outside her apartment door; she pressed her small brown thumb on the bell, and the bell rang shrilly. Markus Werner walked around on the landing, wiping his nose, and said, exhausted, "I'm so beat." The Bali woman turned around and smiled at him. Up to that point she hadn't said a single word, and I could see that her front teeth had been filed down to small stumps and were completely straight. Markus Werner gave her a strained smile and said with exaggerated precision, "Perhaps we had better leave again?" when the door opened and there, in the darkness of the hallway, stood several small children, four or five tiny children in pajamas, barefoot, with tousled hair. They stared at us, and we stared back. The children were a grotesque mixture of their parents, with the heavy, spongy physicality of their father but eyes as dark, small, and distinctive as their mother's. The Bali woman stepped forward into this swarm of pajamas, stuffed animals, and soft children's hands, and the children clung to her and spoke in a foreign language. Markus Werner looked at Christiane. "Did you know about this?" And Christiane, at a loss for the first time, said, "No, I didn't."

Twice in the hallway of the director's apartment, we stepped on hamsters. The hamsters made ghastly noises, and the Bali woman laughed, picked them up, and threw them into one of the apartment's many rooms. The children took one final peek through the crack in the door and then disappeared. The director was nowhere to be seen, and the apartment was dark. The Bali woman led us into the kitchen, lit candles, put water on to boil. Embarrassed, we sat down at the kitchen table; I wanted to sit next to Markus Werner, and Christiane wanted to sit next to me, and so we kept moving around for a while, our sense of shame obvious. Finally we were all sitting. The kitchen was large and warm, and outside the windows it was night; odd garlands were strung across the ceiling; there was a strange smell. We were silent. Christiane avoided my eyes. Like a child, Markus Werner whispered, "What exactly are we doing here?" and nobody answered him. The Bali woman made tea from green leaves, placing small cups, honey, and sugar on the table. She poured with slow, confident movements, smiling all the time, finally sitting down next to Christiane. Markus Werner was looking at a photo that hung on the wall above the table. It showed the director standing next to the Bali woman, in the background palm trees and a too-blue ocean; the director was naked except for a tiny loincloth and an ornament of bananas and flowers on his head. He was glancing sidelong into the camera, obviously embarrassed; the Bali woman was holding his hand, wasn't smiling; the sky above them looked like rain. Markus Werner said, with the same excessive precision, "Your wedding?" and the Bali woman, who had just put her face very close to Christiane's, drew back and nodded. Christiane cleared her throat and put her hands on the table as though she were about to start a meeting. She said, her tone of voice determined and firm, "So where is he?" Markus Werner answered on behalf of the Bali woman, "He's already asleep."

I think we had some good winters together. Was it one or were there several? I don't remember anymore, and you'd say it wasn't important anyway. We had snow and crisp cold weather, and every time I said I really liked being cold you'd look at me as though you understood. We went for walks when the sun was shining. Those long shadows, and you'd break icicles off the tree branches and suck on them. When you fell on the ice I laughed until I had tears in my eyes. We made no promises, and I wanted it that way, too; still—forgive me—I am jealous of all the winters you're going to spend without me. I believe that from now on things will always be the way they were in that kitchen at that table sitting next to Markus Werner, with Christiane and the Bali woman. Morning came. I was so tired. I know that things had never been any different, I just happened to have been wrong one time.

The sky was turning pale outside the windows. It was snowing again, and the snow began to glow. Christiane stood up once, then sat down again. Markus Werner took off his rubber gloves and leaned against me. He kissed me quickly and softly on the neck. The Bali woman saw us and smiled. She said, "There are many jokes in Deutschland." Her voice sounded very bright and childlike, and she stretched out the words and couldn't pronounce the "sch" properly. Markus Werner didn't move. Christiane emitted a short, dry laugh and said irritably, "What?" The Bali woman moved closer to the table, no longer smiling. Very seriously she said, "Jokes. I have learned them all." Markus Werner closed his eyes and said gently, "Why don't you tell us one?" The Bali woman looked up at the garland-decorated ceiling and said, "What is the difference be-

tween a blonde and the *Titanic*?" We didn't say anything.
She waited four, five seconds, then said, "With the *Titanic*
you know how many went down on her." We still didn't
say anything. She looked at us as though she expected an
explanation, a clarification of the joke; she looked terribly
serious, and her eyes were opened wide. Markus Werner
still had his eyes closed, but Christiane's face wore an expression of panic that made me want to laugh. The Bali
woman leaned farther forward and said, "What do you say
to a blonde who falls down the stairs to the basement?"
Again she waited two, three seconds—she actually seemed
to be counting—then she answered herself, " 'Bring back
some beer.' " She said, " 'Bring back some beer' "; the entire time, she looked down at the table with the utmost concentration, as though she were reading the words off its
top. Then she straightened up. She was now sitting ramrod
straight and speaking as though the words had been drilled
into her head—"How do you bury a blonde?"—and she
didn't stop after that. She told one blonde joke after another, ten, twenty, fifty dumb-blonde jokes, and I stared at
her, stared at her strange, concentrated, crazy face; at some
point I no longer understood her at all. She kept speaking
faster and faster, and would ask the question and give the

answer, ask the question and give the answer without pausing. And then I noticed that Christiane was crying—for how long, I don't know. Markus Werner's head slid off my shoulder into my lap. He was asleep, his surprisingly small face nestled in his grandmother's mangy fur. I put my hand under his cheek and supported his head. I felt my heart beating. I felt good.

Then all was quiet. In one of the back rooms an alarm clock rang and a director woke up; outside it had grown light. The Bali woman was silent. She didn't look at all exhausted. She got up and pulled Markus Werner off me and he fell against her; then she gently brushed the coat off his shoulders and moved him over to the kitchen bench. She pushed him down on it, covered him with his coat, stroked his forehead with her small brown hand, then kissed him on the mouth. Christiane and I got up and put on our coats. At the kitchen door we turned once more, and there she was, standing next to the bench in her red dress, looking at us, gravely, directly. She did not say another word, and at that point we left.

Outside it was still cold. An early-morning streetcar drove past us, blue sparks flying off the overhead lines. The city was still quiet and the light was so bright it made me squint. Christiane stopped and tied her hair together at the back of her neck, and I wondered whether I ought to touch her, but I didn't. Her face was all white, and her lips were blue. Then we started to walk, the snow crunching under our feet. I thought that if you had been sleeping you would just now be waking up. You'd wake up and see the frost flowers on your windows.

It is cold. The air smells of snow. Of smoke. Are you listening for something you can't hear, do you have a word on the tip of your tongue that you can't say? Are you restless? Did we meet—just once—and isn't that enough? I'm going to sleep now. Does winter sometimes remind you of something—you don't know of what?

Hunter Johnson Music

THE DAY that something finally does happen after all is the Friday before Easter. Hunter returns toward evening; he's bought canned soup, cigarettes, and white bread at the deli, and picked up the cheapest whiskey at the liquor store; he's tired, a little shaky on his legs. He walks along Eighty-fifth Street, the green plastic deli bag swinging against his knee; on the asphalt the last remnants of March snow are melting into gray, dirty streaks. It's cold, and the neon sign on the Washington-Madison flickers an indecisive "Hotel-Hotel" into the darkness.

Hunter pushes the big swinging door open with the palm of his hand, the warmth drawing him in and taking his breath away. There are black footprints on the green hotel carpet runner. He enters the dim foyer, where dark red silk-covered walls, soft leather-upholstered corner settees, and large crystal chandeliers tell a tale of time irretrievably past; the silk is rippled, the leather corner settees are worn and sagging, the candelabra have lost their sparkling cut-glass pendants, and instead of twelve lightbulbs in each there are only two. The Washington-Madison is no longer a hotel. It is a refuge, a poorhouse for old people, a last dilapidated stop before the end, a place of ghosts. It happens only rarely that an ordinary hotel guest mistakenly finds his way here. As long as no one dies, the rooms are booked for months ahead; when someone dies, the room remains empty for a while, only to house the next old man or woman, for a year or two, or for four days or five.

Hunter shuffles over to the reception desk, where Leach, the hotel owner, is busy picking his nose and going through the personals in the *Village Voice*. Hunter hates Leach. Everybody in the Washington-Madison hates Leach, except for old Miss Gil, who has chosen to offer him her feeble and scarred heart. Leach isn't interested in Miss Gil. Leach is interested in himself, in the *Village Voice* personals—but only the salacious ones, Hunter suspects— and in money. Hunter puts the green deli bag down on the worn reception desk, takes a deep breath, and says, "Mail."

Leach doesn't even look up. He says, "No mail, Mr. Johnson. As always, no mail." Hunter feels his heart trip. It doesn't really trip, it just skips, it skips a beat and hesitates and then goes on beating after all, almost mercifully, as though it wanted to say just kidding. Hunter holds on to the counter with his left hand and says, "I'm sorry, would you mind at least checking to see whether I have any mail."

Leach looks up with the expression of someone who's been repeatedly interrupted during a tremendously important task by something tremendously unimportant, and he points, with a gesture both weary and ritual, at the empty pigeonholes behind him. "Yours is Box Number 93, Mr. Johnson. As you can see, it's empty. Same as every other day."

Hunter stares at the empty slot, at all the other empty slots above and below it; in Box 45 there's Mr. Friedman's chess magazine, and in Box 107 the knitting instructions for Miss Wenders. An unusually large number of knitting instructions. "It looks as though Miss Wenders hasn't picked up her mail for several days, Mr. Leach," Hunter says. "Maybe you should check to see if she's okay."

Leach doesn't answer. Hunter, with a dull feeling of triumph, picks up his plastic bag from the desk and takes the elevator to the fourth floor. The elevator rumbles alarmingly, its routine maintenance is long overdue; on his floor the doors slide open, shaking and creaking. The hall light isn't working. Hunter gropes his way along the wall; ever since Mr. Wright died three weeks ago in Room 95, the room across the hall, he's been alone in this corner of the fourth floor, and he's scared. The red exit sign over the door to the stairway glows weakly. From the bathroom at the end of the hall come sounds of running water, violent nose-blowing and coughing. Hunter shudders. He washes himself as well as he can at the sink in his room, and uses the communal bath with the big old tub as rarely as possible; sadly, he finds old people disgusting, for the most part.

Hunter turns the key in the lock, switches on the light, locks the door behind him. He unpacks the groceries, lies down on the bed, closes his eyes. Tiny green dots dance up and down in the blackness behind his closed lids. The building moves. It is always moving. The floorboards above him creak, somewhere a door slams, the elevator rumbles in the distance. Hunter can hear soft radio music; a telephone rings, somewhere something falls to the floor with a dull thud, the sound of cabs honking rises from the street below. Hunter likes these noises. He likes the

Washington-Madison in a certain sad, resigned way. He likes his room, for which he pays four hundred dollars a month; he replaced the twenty-watt bulb in the ceiling fixture with a sixty-watt one and put up blue curtains at the windows. He's arranged his books on the bookshelf, the tape player and tapes on the bureau, and he has hung two photographs above the bed. There's a chair for visitors who never come, and a telephone that never rings. Next to the sink a refrigerator, and on the refrigerator a hot plate. All the rooms are furnished like this. Once a week the bed linens are changed; but when he moved in, Hunter insisted on doing it himself. He doesn't like the idea of the chambermaid rummaging around among his books, papers, and tapes.

Hunter turns over on his back, pushes aside the curtain at the window next to the bed, and stares out; the grille of the fire escape slices the dark sky into small squares. He falls asleep, then wakes up again and sits on the edge of the bed, glancing briefly at the brown, patterned rug between his feet. He gets up. It's going to snow one more time this March, he can feel it in his bones, a chilly, unpleasant prickling. But his tiredness is gone: the room is warm, there's banging in the heating pipes, and far away at the end of the hall, Miss Gil is singing to herself in a thin, high voice. Hunter smiles briefly. He heats a can of soup on the hot plate, pours himself a glass of whiskey, and eats in front of the television. The newscaster on CNN reports in an apathetic voice that a boy has shot three employees in a McDonald's in East New York, Brooklyn. The boy appears on the television screen. He is black, and seventeen years old maybe; three police officers parade him before the cameras. A voice from nowhere asks about his motive. The boy looks directly into the cameras; he seems completely normal. He explains that he had ordered a Big Mac without pickles. Specifically: no pickles. But he'd gotten a Big Mac *with* pickles.

Hunter turns off the television. Out in the hall, the door to Room 95 slams shut. Hunter turns his head and listens, irritated; silence. He washes his plates and pot, pours himself another glass of whiskey, and stands in front of his tapes, undecided. Time for music. Time for music, just like every night; time for a cigarette, time for time. What else should he do if not listen to music? Hunter rubs a hand over his eyes and briefly feels for his heartbeat. His heart is beating quietly and sluggishly. Maybe Mozart. Or better still, Beethoven. Schubert, as always, is too sad. Bach. Johann Sebastian Bach, *The Well-Tempered Clavier, Book I*. Hunter slides the tape into the player and pushes the play button. There is a soft hissing sound. He sits down on the chair by the window and lights a cigarette.

Glenn Gould's playing is slow, concentrated and lingering. Now and then Hunter can hear him singing along softly, sometimes breathing heavily: Hunter likes that, it's a personal touch. He sits on the chair, listening. While listening to music, he can think well or not think at all; either way, it's nice. Cabs honk in the distance. Miss Gil has stopped singing, or perhaps Glenn Gould is louder than Miss Gil. Outside Hunter's door a floorboard creaks. The board creaks noisily. The board had always creaked noisily whenever Mr. Wright stood outside his door, looking for cigarettes or whiskey or company. Mr. Wright is dead. He died three weeks ago, the only person ever to stand in front of Hunter's door.

Hunter stares at the door with wide-open eyes. The doorknob, does not turn, as it would in the movies, but there's another creak. Hunter's heart suddenly starts beating surprisingly fast. New York is a crime-ridden city.

Nobody would take him seriously if he were to yell for help. Leach would pretend he'd forgotten the police emergency number. Hunter gets up. He tiptoes to the door, his heart now skipping beats. He puts his hand on the doorknob, takes a deep breath, and flings the door wide open.

The girl stands in the red light of the exit sign. Hunter sees small feet with curled toes, a mosquito bite scratched open on the left ankle, a tiny bit of dirt under the big toenail. Her bathrobe is frayed at the hem, blue with white appliquéd rabbits on the pockets. She has the robe tied tightly around her waist, and under her arm she has a towel and a bottle of shampoo. Her right hand holds the bathrobe closed at her throat: her lips are thin and she seems agitated. Water drips steadily from her wet hair onto the brown hall carpet. She squints and peers past Hunter into his room. Below her left eye there's a small birthmark. Involuntarily Hunter looks down at himself and notices that he can't see his belt buckle because his belly protrudes above it. The girl says something like, "The music."

Hunter pulls the door toward him and tries to block her view of the room. He can hear Miss Gil singing again, she's singing, "Honey pie, you are making me crazy," and for some reason, he finds that embarrassing. The girl says something like, "I'm sorry, the music," pronouncing the words awkwardly, like a child, at the same time rubbing the toes of her right foot against her left calf.

Hunter gets goosebumps. He steps out into the hall and pulls the door shut behind him, saying, "What do you mean?" The girl draws back and screws up her thin lips. Hunter feels his hand trembling on the doorknob. The girl, transferring the towel and shampoo bottle from her right arm to the left, says, "Are you watching TV or are you listening to music?" Hunter stares at her. He has a vague memory of some TV show he has seen, but he doesn't understand her; she's speaking in a code he can't crack: does he watch TV or does he listen to music. What does that mean?

She says, "Television or music? Commercial—ad—or really music?"

Hunter repeats hesitantly, "Really music," and the girl, impatient now, bounces up and down on her toes and says, "Bach."

Hunter says, "Yes, Bach. *The Well-Tempered Clavier.* Glenn Gould."

She says, "Well then. So you *are* listening to music."

Hunter takes a deep breath, aware of his belly distending even more, but he immediately feels better. Of course he's listening to music. He wants to go back to the beginning, to the first question, and he has a hard time hiding his confusion from her: he imagines he looks like an old fool. He repeats, this time with more self-assurance, "What do you mean?" The girl answers slowly, sounding like a teacher whose pupil has finally understood, "I stopped in front of your door to listen to the music."

Hunter smiles uncomprehendingly, thinks of dogs baring their teeth. Miss Gil sings "I'm in love but I'm lazy," and he feels an urge to wring her wrinkled neck, as they do to ducks in the comics. He giggles. The girl giggles too, and says, "She's not all there, is she?" Hunter stops giggling and says gruffly, "She's old."

The girl raises her left eyebrow. Hunter turns the doorknob, ready to retreat to his room, and says self-consciously, "Yes, well."

Taking a resolute breath and shifting from one foot to the other, the girl says three sentences in a row. Hunter has to make a tremendous effort to concentrate. She says, "You know, I'm here only temporarily. Room 95. It was nice to hear your music; you see, somebody swiped my tape player."

Before she's even finished saying "tape player" Hunter says, "Who?" He feels that he has to gain time: this is all too much for him, she is way too young for this hotel, she talks so funny. She says, "These guys at Grand Central, they stole my backpack and my tape player and all my tapes, and now I can't listen to music anymore. Which is bad. Nothing works without music." She looks at Hunter expectantly and attentively.

Hunter says, "I'm sorry to hear that," and peers down the dark hallway looking for help. Miss Gil has stopped singing, and he entertains the faint hope that she'll come to the elevator and interrupt this situation. Miss Gil doesn't come. The girl—Hunter senses that she is observing him—says, "Do you live here?" with peculiar emphasis. Hunter turns to face her again. The expression around her mouth is almost cruel, and her upper body is bent forward possessively; water is still dripping from her hair.

"Yes," says Hunter. "I mean, I . . ." He breaks off in mid-sentence and is briefly tempted to leave her standing there, to go back into his room and slam the door in her face.

"This is a weird hotel, isn't it?" the girl asks, one of her hands now in the pocket of her bathrobe making the rabbit appliqué bulge obscenely. Hunter feels completely exhausted. He longs for Glenn Gould, for the blue curtains of his room, for sleep. He is no longer accustomed to this sort of thing; he is no longer accustomed to meeting people, to having conversations. He says, "Excuse me," and the girl sighs dramatically. She takes her room key out of her bathrobe pocket and smiles reassuringly at Hunter. "Do you want to get dinner or something? Maybe tomorrow night, you could show me a good restaurant and tell me a little about the city, you know what I mean." Hunter remembers that he hasn't eaten out for years, that he doesn't know any good restaurants, that he can't tell her anything about the city, that he knows nothing at all. He says, "Of course, that'd be nice"—he would have said, "Of course, that'd be nice," to anything—and the girl grins and says, "Well then, tomorrow night at eight; I'll pick you up. Good night."

Hunter nods. He watches her back as she unlocks her door, the terrycloth of her bathrobe wet and dark along her spine. He looks at her closed door and hears her humming behind it, hears her brushing her teeth. He sees the light under the door go out. He is not sure he'll have the strength to go back into his room.

❈

The next morning he wakes up because in the hall outside the communal bathroom Miss Gil is arguing with Mr. Dobrian. Miss Gil's high, shrill voice breaks into his room; her voice is shaking and triumphant. "You pig!" Miss Gil yells. "You pig, you filthy pervert, you jerk! To come bursting into the bathroom when women are bathing; I'm going to tell Mr. Leach!" Hunter hears Mr. Dobrian's fragile, tired, old-man's voice: "But you purposely leave the door unlocked, Miss Gil; if you would lock it this couldn't happen!" It was the same every day. Miss Gil never locked the door; someone would go in, see her standing there naked, wrinkled and shriveled, leave again quickly, disgusted, then have to endure her endless ranting. Hunter sighs and pulls the blanket over his head, sleep slipping away from him like a cloth, the face of the girl with the wet hair appearing briefly before him. He thinks of their date, of having dinner with her that night, and he feels an ache in his stomach. He shouldn't have done it. He shouldn't have agreed to it. He doesn't know what to talk about; she seems a bit naive, and it's been a long time since he's had any thoughts about women. What a crazy idea, to think of going out with a stranger, a girl much too young for him, and in his condition no less; a grotesque idea, ridiculous.

Hunter sits up. He looks briefly through the window at the sky, which is gray and overcast. Easter Saturday, a free day, a terribly free night. Miss Gil's voice, still nagging, is moving farther down the hall. Hunter gets up, washes, dresses, pulls open the window, and stares briefly down at the wet, early-morning street. A fat kid carrying a box under his arm trips and falls, gets up again, walks on. Hunter takes the elevator to the ground floor, hurries to reach the front door, hurries to escape Leach's voice, but is too slow.

"Mr. Johnson!" Leach's voice is both enticing and offensive. Hunter stops in mid-stride and turns halfway toward the reception desk. He doesn't answer.

"Have you seen her already, Mr. Johnson?"

"Have I seen whom already?" says Hunter.

"The girl, Mr. Johnson. The girl I put in Room 95 for you!" Leach succeeds in placing such a loathsome emphasis on the word "girl" that it sends a cold shiver down Hunter's back.

"No," he says, his hand already on the glass pane of the swinging door. "I haven't seen her yet."

Leach triumphantly calls after him, "Oh, but you're lying, Mr. Johnson! She told me herself, this morning, that she talked to you. She was very impressed, Mr. Johnson!"

Hunter lets the swinging door slam shut, steps out into the cool street air, and spits. The girl seems to be more stupid than he thought. He walks along Eighty-fifth Street to Broadway. Even though it's Saturday and early morning, the traffic's already heavy. The lights flash green and red, and crowds stream out of the stores. A nightmarish giant Easter rabbit stands on the corner of Seventy-fifth, throwing chocolate eggs into the crowd. Hunter walks around aimlessly, absorbed in his own thoughts; the sky is heavy with rain and there's an icy crackling in the air. People bump into him; at the corner of Broadway and Sixty-fifth he stands around for five minutes until the newspaper vendor points out to him that the light has just turned green for the third time. He turns and starts walking uptown again, heading toward the park, and buys a sandwich and a coffee at a little coffee shop. A tattered beggar approaches people and tugs at their shopping bags. Hunter steers clear of him but bumps instead into an enormously fat black woman. He excuses himself, and she smiles and says, "No problem, honey." The crazy man in front of

Filene's Basement yells, "Too much electricity!" He's been standing there as long as Hunter can remember, yelling, "Too much electricity makes people crazy!" Passersby laugh and throw dimes at his feet, but he never picks them up. Outside Zabar's, workers eat salads out of plastic containers, sitting next to each other, their feet equal distances apart. Hunter turns into a side street. It's quieter here, green wreaths with yellow ribbons hang on the front doors of four-story brick town houses. In the park he sits down to drink the coffee, cold by now, and eats the sandwich. The day glides by. Around noon a gentle rain begins to fall.

Hunter continues to sit there. Pigeons peck at rat-poison-yellow grains, a girl on Roller Blades whizzes by, black nannies holding the hands of sickly and haughty-looking white children sit down next to him. Hunter's eyes remain fixed on the pebbles between his feet, gray pebbles with white dots. He feels an uneasiness in his joints, in his hands, that he has never felt before. It's an uneasiness that has nothing to do with the snow, although yesterday's chilly prickling has increased. The park, which usually makes him feel calm and tired, today seems inaccessible, unfriendly. An old Asian woman pokes around in the garbage cans with a wire coat hanger, babbling to herself; then, morosely and without any booty, she disappears among the trees on the other side of the lawn. In front of Hunter's bench a pigeon keels over, claws twitching, then is still. Hunter moves to the next bench. The clouds part, revealing a pale, dull March sky. Perplexed, he thinks, Time. And time, and then he doesn't think about anything. He leaves the park as long shadows begin to stretch out between the benches, and walks back to Broadway, the evening traffic just as idiotically heavy as in the morning. He turns in to Eighty-third Street; the parking garage near the corner recklessly spits out cars. Hunter crosses to the other side of the street, and, feeling cold, thrusts his hands deeper into his coat pockets. There's a light in Lenny's store.

Hunter carefully pushes the small glass door open. He gets tangled up in the felt curtain behind it and trips in the dark. He can hear Lenny laughing softly. He disentangles himself from the curtain and laughs, too, much against his will; Lenny is sitting in his dusty rocking chair behind the cash register, holding his hand in front of his mouth like a girl. "Stop that," Hunter says. Lenny, exaggerating, takes a deep breath, and disappears as he reaches down to a shelf below the cash register. He reappears with a bottle of whiskey and two glasses. It's warm in the store. Filaments of dust flicker in the yellow light, and there's a smell of paper and damp wood. Lenny's rocking chair is back there among books, picture frames, Halloween masks, moldy little boxes and bolts of fabric, plastic flowers, canned food, yellowed postcards. Umbrellas, wigs, baseball bats. Hunter brushes a stack of ancient lottery tickets off a lawn chair and sits down. Lenny pours the whiskey; dust seems to have settled in the folds of his face, and the eyes behind his thick lenses have a moist gleam. He says, "You were here just the day before yesterday, Johnson." Hunter smiles and says, "I'm leaving right away." Lenny doesn't answer and rocks his chair back into the darkness of the store. The whiskey tastes salty. Somewhere water is dripping; the noise of the street is far away. Hunter is beginning to feel warm. He no longer knows why he's here. He no longer wants to know why he's here, he just wants to go on sitting here the way he always does—quietly, for a long time, without a reason—then leave. Lenny, watching him, senses this. Lenny is clever. He clears his throat, spits the mucus into an old tin bowl, and says, "Johnson. You don't mean you actually want to buy something, do you?"

Hunter sits up straight. The lawn chair creaks, and he can hear the blood roaring in his ears. He says, "I need a tape player. Nothing special, just one of those little portable ones, I thought maybe you'd have something like that." He tries to give his voice a casual, carefree note. Behind his glasses Lenny's eyes become small, narrow slits. "But you already have a tape player, Johnson. Why do you need another one?"

Hunter clears his throat. He would like to evade Lenny's gaze, and already regrets having asked at all; he's unable to lie. He says, "I want it for a gift." Lenny looks away. He rocks back and forth, slowly, idly, whistling briefly to himself, shaking his head. Hunter takes a careful breath. Lenny gets up and disappears into the depths of the store. Glass shatters, books fall, dust rises. Lenny coughs and curses, tugs at something, comes back; in his knotty, brown-flecked hands he holds a small, almost dainty tape player with a silver tape deck.

Hunter is perspiring. The collar of his winter coat is chafing his neck and the wool scarf itches. Hunter finds it unbearably hot. Lenny puts the tape player next to the cash register and busies himself wiping it with a dust rag. He looks concerned. He actually looks concerned. Hunter turns his head away and moves his garden chair back into the murky twilight. Lenny leans forward and says, "You know that I don't sell things anymore. I just sit here. I don't sell anything anymore."

"Yes," Hunter says weakly. "I know."

Lenny sighs indulgently, spits again, then chortles softly. "I'm surprised at you, Johnson. I'm really surprised. I guess you're not planning to give this player to Leach. Or to Miss Gil." He eyes Hunter through his thick lenses, a dust flake quivering on his bald head. "Now, Johnson. Who's this player for?" Hunter makes no reply. He feels the weariness unfolding between his shoulder blades and wipes the sweat from his forehead with the back of his hand. Lenny comes out from behind the cash register, kicks over two piles of books, and puts the little player in Hunter's lap. He says, "Take it. I don't need it anymore. If you change your mind, bring it back. Johnson . . ." Lenny breaks off and shuffles back to the rocking chair. He sits down and looks at his spit in the tin bowl. Hunter touches the silver tape deck. Cool and smooth. He wishes Lenny would say something else. He would like Lenny to take the player back again, wishes he were back in his room, in his bed, in the darkness. Lenny is silent. Water is dripping.

Somewhere the rustling of paper. Hunter gets up, takes the tape player, and goes to the door. He says, "Thanks a lot." "No problem," says Lenny from the depths of his rocking chair; Hunter stands there with his back to him, waiting, feeling his heart beating. Lenny says, "Johnson?" Hunter clears his throat. Lenny says, "Will you come again, tomorrow, the day after tomorrow?" Hunter says, "Sure." He pushes the felt curtain aside, opens the small glass door, and smells the snow. "I hope so," Lenny says, as Hunter steps out into the cold, dark street.

At the Washington-Madison Leach is behind the reception desk, reading the *Village Voice*. He doesn't look up. Hunter, the tape player concealed under his coat, takes the elevator up, tiptoes through the hall, unlocks the door to his room, and locks it behind him. His knees are shaking. It is six forty-five. It is quiet in the hallway and in Room 95.

An hour. Another hour, then she'll be here. Hunter sits on the chair by the window and stares at his closet. He's wrapped the tape player in newspaper and tied a woolen thread around it. It's now sitting on the table, and it looks ridiculous. Hunter turns away, then walks over to the closet to take out a suit. It is black and smells of dust, worn at the knees and elbows, the collar shiny. The last time he wore it was to Mr. Wright's funeral, it's his Washington-Madison funeral suit, and the thought that he's going to wear it tonight makes Hunter explode in hysterical laughter. He feels sick. He feels sick to his stomach, around his heart, and in his throat; he throws the suit on the bed and runs hot water into the sink. The girl isn't going to get him to wash in the communal bathroom. The girl won't get him to wash at all, he'll just shave and comb his hair; it's all hopeless anyway. In front of the mirror above the sink Hunter opens his eyes slowly. The mirror is small, misted over with steam; Hunter looks at his face in the merciful white steam. He shaves carefully, but his hands are shaking too much. He cuts his chin slightly, making a little blood ooze out, its color a strange, sickly red. Hunter gags. He takes a deep breath, runs cold water over his wrists, counts. He can smell the shaving foam, the soap, peppermint. He staunches the blood with a scrap of newspaper, puts on his suit; the sleeves are too short, a button is missing. Hunter feels as though he is in a dream. Sleepwalking. Almost apathetic. He lights a cigarette, hitches up his trousers, and sits down on the edge of the bed. He coughs. It's seven forty-five. He waits.

The square of sky between the grille of the fire escape turns pale, then black. It's raining a little. The clock on his night table is ticking, and the water gurgles in the heating pipes. For a moment the building lurches in a strange un-accustomed motion. Like a ship, Hunter thinks. Like a ship, it has cast off, has left shore a long time ago, I just didn't notice. All the sounds, as though coming from far away. The hand of the clock wanders around in a circle, drawing the hours and hours. The girl is not coming; of course she's not coming. Hunter lies on his bed and smiles, looks at the ceiling, water stains up there, cracks in the plaster— disappointed relief. After all, what would it have been like? What would it have looked like, this evening in a good restaurant, the mocking smiles of the waiters, the coins in his pocket, his trembling hands, his difficulties swallowing. She would have had to do the talking. He would have been unable to speak, would only have listened to the sound of his heart, the beats getting faster and faster, until . . . Hunter lies on his bed and smiles. Time, he thinks. Time and time. The clock says eleven. He pulls the blanket up over his knees and rolls over on his side, his gaze touching the objects in the room, their worn, soft familiarity. It is warm. His tiredness is heavy and pleasant.

Around midnight the door to Room 95 slams shut. Hunter hadn't heard the girl, her light springy step in the dark hall, probably a sound too unfamiliar. He sits up and listens; everything remains still. He gets up, feels dizzy, blackness in front of his eyes, then it passes. He takes his suit off again, the jacket, the pants, wrinkled now and crumpled, carefully hangs them up in the closet. He stands in front of his tapes, Mozart and Bach, sad Schubert and soft, gentle Satie. The Portuguese fado songs for Sundays and the voice of Janis Joplin for which he is too old, has always been too old. Sometimes, in a good mood, Astor Piazzolla. And that American, that big, crazy, ugly bird from California whose "Jersey Girl" is the only song he has ever heard him sing, but he'd loved it. And again Mozart and Schumann, between them a recording by Stevens, where did that come from? Hunter slides his hand over the tape cases, shakes his head, smiles, confused. Tango music.

Callas arias. Music and time, time, *Die Winterreise*, the strange African songs he bought at the flea market in Tompkins Square seven years ago, or was it eight? or ten? Hunter doesn't cry. He turns the cases over in his hands. He can't read his own writing anymore, jazz and poetry, the voice of Truman Capote. Then he starts packing them up, getting a small shoebox out of the closet, putting the tapes into it, very neatly, side by side; some have no writing on them, let her find out for herself. Also the Glenn Gould cassette that was in the player. That one too, Hunter doesn't forget a thing. The girl knocks on the door, it's already late, so late, much too late. Hunter puts the cover on the shoebox and places the box on top of the little package containing the tape player. He opens the door a crack and slides both out into the hall.

The girl says, "Please." She wedges her foot into the door. Hunter pushes it back with both hands, says, "Happy Easter," and pushes the door shut. The girl, on the other side of the door, says, "Please," once more, says, "I'm sorry. I know. I'm way too late." Hunter squats on the floor and doesn't answer. He can hear her breathe. He can hear her pick up the two small boxes, lift the cover off the shoebox, tear the newspaper off the little package. She says, "Oh." The tape cases clatter softly against each other, she says, "Oh my God," then starts to cry. Hunter puts his hands over his face and presses his thumbs into his closed eyelids until there's an explosion of color. The girl in the hall cries. Maybe she's vain. Maybe disappointed. Hunter leans his head against the door. His head is so heavy, and he doesn't want to listen anymore, but he listens anyway. The girl says, "You don't have to do this." Hunter says, very softly—he doesn't know if she can hear him, but, after all, he's just speaking to himself—"I know. But that's the way I want it." The girl says, "Thank you." Hunter nods. He hears her coat rustle; it's probably a plastic coat, maybe green. She pushes against the door, but it doesn't yield. She asks, "You won't open it just one more time?" Hunter shakes his head. She says, "Just one question, one last question, would you answer that?" "Yes," Hunter says, uttering it into the crack between the door and the wall; her mouth must be somewhere around there, he guesses, her thin-lipped, nervous, restless mouth. She says, "I only want to know why you live here, why, can you tell me that?" Hunter places his face against the crack: there's a little draft, and cold air enters, coolness. He closes his eyes again, says, "Because I can leave. Pack my suitcases, any day, any morning, pull the door shut behind me, go." The girl is silent. Then she says, "Go where, though?" Hunter instantly replies, "That question is completely irrelevant." The pressure against the door subsides. The plastic coat rustles. The girl seems to be getting up, the cool draft from the crack is gone. "Yes," she says. "I understand. Good night." "Good night," Hunter says; he knows she will have finished packing her suitcase, the tape player, his music and will have left before it's light outside.

Camera Obscura

THE ARTIST is very short. Sometimes Marie wonders whether she's still in her right mind: the artist is way too short. She says to herself, You've lost it; maybe because fall is coming, or because the old restlessness is returning. The chill in her back, the rain?

The artist really is short. At least three heads shorter than Marie. He is famous. Everybody knows him, at least everyone in Berlin does. He creates art with a computer and has written two books, and sometimes he talks on late-night radio shows. On top of that the artist is ugly. He has a very small, proletarian head and is very dark: some people say he has Spanish blood. His mouth is incredibly small. Nonexistent. His eyes, though, are beautiful, black and large; usually when he talks he holds his hand in front of his face so that you only see those eyes. The artist's clothes are awful. He wears torn jeans—a child's size, Marie guesses—and always a green jacket, always sneakers. A black leather band is knotted around his left wrist. Some people say that regardless of all this, the artist is incredibly intelligent.

Marie wants something from the artist. What it is she doesn't really know. Perhaps the glamour of his fame. Perhaps to look even more beautiful beside an ugly person. Perhaps to penetrate and destroy his seeming impassiveness. Marie asks herself, in all seriousness, whether she's still okay. Don't they look somewhat ridiculous together? Marie had always wanted to be only with beautiful people. It's weird to have to look down at a man. It's weird to imagine what it would be like if . . . Still, that's what Marie wants.

They kiss on the very first evening. Or rather, Marie kisses the artist. Suddenly he's standing in front of her, at this party, among all the Berlin celebrities, and Marie can't decide on which of the celebrities to cast her long, long gaze first. The artist offers himself. Suddenly he is standing in front of her with those beautiful black eyes, and Marie, having seen him on television, recognizes him immediately. He keeps pouring vodka into her glass and asks difficult questions: "What does being happy mean to you?" "Have you ever betrayed someone?" "Do you feel bad if you've achieved something only because of your looks?"

Marie drinks the vodka, hesitates, says: "Happiness is always the moment before. The second before the moment in which I actually should be happy. In that second I am happy and don't know it. I've betrayed a lot of people, I think. And I like achieving things because of my looks."

The artist stares at her. Marie stares back. She's good at that. The people around her are growing restless; the artist is really too short and too ugly. More out of spite than solidarity Marie bends down, takes the artist's head into both her hands, and kisses him on the mouth. He kisses her back, of course. Then Marie gives him her phone number and leaves, realizing only outside in the cold and clear night air how drunk she really is.

The artist waits three days, then calls her. Did he really—wait, that is? Marie assumes so. They spend an evening at a bar, where Marie is freezing and keeps having spells of weakness because the artist is constantly looking at her and doesn't want to talk. One morning they go for a walk in the park, the artist wearing stylish sunglasses that Marie likes. For one whole afternoon they sit in a café, and Marie tells him a little about herself. Otherwise she is silent. The artist says he doesn't like conversations on a meta-level.

Marie doesn't know what "meta-level" is supposed to mean. Whenever she goes to meet him she puts on the only pair of flats she owns. The difference in their heights embarrasses her. It is fall. Dying wasps tumble through the open window into Marie's room. She feels cold and wears gloves; the days are already short, and she is often tired. Sometimes she tilts her head back and tries to laugh effervescently, but it doesn't come out right. One day the artist asks whether she would like to drive to the Baltic Sea with him some time, for a couple of days. Marie says yes and thinks of places like Ahlbeck, Fischland, and Hiddensee, of a long white wintry beach, of shells and a calm sea. She doesn't think of the artist. She stands at her window, holding a cup of cold tea, and stares out into the street. She is confused nowadays, puts lighted cigarettes between her lips the wrong way around, leaves the water running, loses her keys. Once the artist calls her and actually says, "I love you." Marie is squatting on the floor, the phone clamped between her head and shoulder, looking into the mirror. She closes her eyes slowly, and slowly opens them again. The artist isn't saying anything else now, but she hears him breathing, softly, regularly, calmly. He is not nervous. Marie isn't either. Again she says, "Yes," and is surprised that the answer comes so quickly. The artist hangs up.

When Marie thinks of his eyes she feels an ache in her back. His eyes really are beautiful. She is not *waiting* for him to call, she *knows* he'll call. The artist seems to be quite content with his dwarfishness. He emphasizes it by moving in a fidgety and clownish way, walking like a tin soldier, sometimes doing a handstand in the middle of the street, making faces, doing magic tricks by putting coins into his ear and retrieving them from his nose. Since the kiss at the party he hasn't touched Marie. Nor she him. When they say good-bye, he acts as though he's about to put his hand on her arm, but at the last moment he always draws it away again. He asks her, "What does it mean when you look at me for such a long time?" Marie answers, "Closeness, aggression, also sexuality, and consent." She doesn't know whether that's true. The artist can't smile. When he thinks he's smiling, he's only squeezing his eyes together into narrow slits and pulling up the corners of his mouth. Marie doesn't find this convincing, and she tells him so, triumph in her voice. "Could be," says the artist. For the first time he looks hurt.

In a café, one night, when Marie is already very drunk, she asks him whether he has ever considered going to bed with her. She knows it's wrong, but she can't help herself, she's been wanting to ask him for days. The artist says, "I guess there have been women I've made a greater effort with." Marie is indignant, crosses her arms over her chest and decides not to say another word. The artist drinks his wine, smokes, looks at her, and says, "You'd better leave now." Marie rides home on her bike, furious.

Later she calls him. "I don't like being observed by you," says the artist: nevertheless he says he is willing to see her again. In a way he reminds Marie of an animal. A small animal. A black, hairy, creepy little monkey. She puts her low-heeled shoes into the closet, puts on high-heeled boots, and for the first time rides her bike over to his apartment.

The artist opens the door, but only after she has rung the bell three times. He's wearing his sneakers, torn jeans, his black sweater. He once told Marie that he always buys fifteen small-sized sweaters at a time and dyes them all black. It's warm in the apartment. Strangely neat and tidy. The walls are painted orange, with huge quantities of books, CDs, records. "Would you like some tea?" the artist asks. Yes, says Marie sitting down at his desk—which isn't near the window but against the back wall—on the only chair in the room. Postcards, newspaper cartoons, photos, letters are pinned to the wall above the desk. Small pieces of paper, layered, one on top of the other. The artist somewhere in the sunny South, a blond, chubby-cheeked child in his arms. Theater programs, a book review, neatly cut out. A strip of passport photos of the artist, shot from above because of his size, the flash creating a white spot on his forehead. A sentence in large letters on yellow paper: "In times of betrayal landscapes are beautiful." In the kitchen the artist is clattering around with the cups. Marie, biting her lower lip, is self-conscious and nervous. She hears his approaching steps rustle on the cork matting and turns around to face him, putting on a wooden smile. The artist sets the cups on the glass surface of the desk and asks, "Music?" Marie shrugs and clings to her cup. The artist puts a CD into the player. There is a crackling in the loudspeakers, P. J. Harvey's voice is heard from very far away—*Is that all there is?* Depression music, Marie thinks, wondering whether she should say it out loud. The artist circles around her, looking very self-satisfied and sure of himself and observing her with a mocking expression. Marie clears her throat. The artist says, "How about turning on the computer?" Marie replies, "I don't know anything about computers." The artist says amiably, "That doesn't matter."

He switches on his computer. It hums softly, the black of the screen turning a bright clear blue. A smiling miniature computer appears and in the left margin of the screen various small icons open up. Marie twists her hands in her lap and feels very uncomfortable. The artist taps on the keys and circles around gently with the mouse; he pulls out a fist-sized gray sphere from behind the computer. In its center is a gleaming black eye. He places the sphere in the middle of the desk and adjusts it so the black gleaming eye is focused directly on Marie's face. Marie stares at the sphere and the artist circles softly with the mouse. The screen turns white. Now, in its upper left corner, tiny light- and dark-gray squares appear, a grid of small dots spreading silently and quickly over the surface

of the screen. The parting in Marie's hair, Marie's forehead, Marie's eyebrows, her eyes, her nose, mouth, chin,
neck, the top of her breasts, an eerie black-and-white
Marie-face.

"That's hideous," Marie says. With a time delay and
silently, the Marie-face on the screen repeats the words,
"That's hideous." It opens and closes its eyes and
mouth, fishlike, terrible, dreadful. "The image hasn't
fully formed yet," the artist says. He keys in something,
and the Marie-face becomes sharper, its contours clearer,
and in the background the bookshelves on the right-
hand wall of the room come into view, the window, the
sky outside, gray on the screen, gray also in reality. "You
can shoot almost anything with it," the artist says,
smiling unconvincingly and pleasantly at Marie. Marie
smiles back, unconvinced. It is quiet. Marie endures the
stare of the artist, who is no longer smiling. A third,
black and beautiful eye has grown between his eyebrows.
Marie blinks and the eye disappears again. The computer
whirrs. Marie doesn't dare look at the screen, afraid of
the gray and eerie Marie-face. The cork matting rustles
because the artist is now coming toward her. Marie
presses her back against the chair and stares fixedly into

the artist's eyes, as though this might help keep the terror at bay. The artist puts his right hand on Marie's cheek; the hand is cool and soft. Marie briefly closes her eyes. Then his face is directly in front of hers, Marie stops breathing, and he kisses her on the lips. Marie is very sober. He probably is, too. The kiss appears on the computer screen, with a time delay and silent, a gray repetition of an instant. Now Marie looks, past the face, past the closed eyes of the artist, at the screen on which his face snuggles up to hers, replacing her face: she opens her eyes, in black and white.

Something is turning in Marie's head. The artist takes a deep breath, presses against Marie, pushes his hand around to the back of her neck, down her back, inside her dress. Marie concentrates. Instead of seeing herself as usual from above, from a sort of bird's-eye view, she looks at the screen, at this silent, strange entwining of two human beings, and it is bizarre. It is warm in the room. Small pieces of paper hang in layers above the desk, the artist somewhere in the sunny south, a blond, chubby-cheeked child in his arms. Too bad, Marie thinks, that you can see things for the first time only once.

The artist pulls Marie off the chair and onto the floor. At some point Marie is wearing nothing but her high-heeled boots, and then not even those. On the computer screen you see a wall of bookshelves, the back of an empty chair, a window, and outside, a darker sky.

This Side of the Oder

K OBERLING IS standing on the hill when they arrive. The hill is a mound of soil that Koberling piled up with his own hands in the middle of the garden two years ago. Back then Constance had laughed and called it Field Marshal Hill; he had countered with Napoleon Hill, and the name stuck. From there he has a view of the lawn, the veranda, the shady entrance to the kitchen, and the rolling fields beyond which the Oder flows.

Koberling is standing on Napoleon Hill, smoking a cigarette; he shades his eyes with one hand and stares toward the horizon. Somewhere over there is the Oder, hidden in its riverbed. Somewhere over there, too, is Constance, taking her daily walk in the afternoon heat. The child is sleeping in the kitchen, exhausted by the summer. Koberling brushes away a wasp and thinks of fall.

The sound of a car's engine comes creeping up the sandy road like an illusion. Koberling turns his head, listening, and squints: no, no car ever comes driving up the sandy road except his own. It's not an illusion, though. The sound of a diesel engine, a crunch of pebbles, Koberling beside himself, his heart pounding. Out of the corner of his right eye he catches sight of an old Mercedes. Koberling remains motionless, wants to be invisible, thinks, Keep on going. The Mercedes stops in front of the garden gate. Dust from the road swirls up, the door opens on the passenger side, and Anna climbs out. Koberling recognizes her immediately. She looks the same as before, same as back then, only bigger, taller, a grown-up child. "Koberling!" she shouts, and stalks around the car in high heels, stopping at the garden gate. She's wearing a red dress and is deeply tanned. The window on the driver's side is being rolled down and a young man with matted hair sticks his head out, yawning. Koberling has butterflies in his stomach and says very softly and viciously, "Pothead."

"Hey!" Anna shouts. "We've just come back from Poland. We don't have any money left, and we thought we could stay with you, just for a few days. Koberling! Do you remember me?"

Koberling crushes the cigarette under his foot and comes down off the hill. "I remember you. I can hear you. No need to shout like that."

Anna's hand is on the handle of the garden gate, and the pothead is languidly peeling himself out of the car. Now Koberling can see that he's wearing unbelievably dirty jeans. Max calls from the kitchen in a sleepy and cracked child's voice, and Koberling knows that the light is falling on the little bed they've made for him on the window seat and that the flies are circling the lamp; suddenly he feels weak, overwhelmed. Where is Constance, he thinks, Constance who could be taking all this off my shoulders, because I don't want any visitors and especially no potheads.

He wipes the sweat from his upper lip and takes the pebbled path toward the garden gate. The crunch of the pebbles is surprisingly loud. Anna, Koberling thinks. Anna. You and your clown father, ridiculous buffoon, circus fool. When you were a child I once slapped you because you jumped on my back while I was meditating on the lawn in front of your house. When you were a child you didn't matter to me. I sat in the kitchen with your clown father and we talked and drank ourselves under the table. At best you got on my nerves with your chocolate-smeared mouth, and you still get on my nerves now.

Koberling pushes back the bolt and pulls open the garden gate, smiling like an idiot, sweating incredibly. "Wow, Koberling," Anna says, grinning, and follows this with a sort of "Oh." "Wow, Koberling. It must be years since the last time we saw each other. Years!"

"Yes," Koberling says, "years."

The pothead takes two lethargic steps toward Koberling and extends a dirty hand. Koberling doesn't take it. He remains protectively near the gate, as though this would make them understand, as though the mere presence of the silent and tense bastion of his body would make it clear to them that they should leave. That visitors were not welcome here. That old friendships no longer counted. But they do not understand. They stand there and stare. Koberling turns and takes the gravel path back to the veranda and, speaking into the blue, says, "You can stay if you want to. There's a guest room in the attic."

Toward evening Constance returns from her walk, no later than usual but for Koberling later than ever before. He's sitting on the veranda with Anna and the pothead, whose name he doesn't want to know, smoking one cigarette after the other. Max squats on the floor in front of the pothead, listening to his jumbled stories. Extraterrestrials, Druids, New Guinea, the end of the world. Max's mouth is wide open, a rope of spittle runs down his chin, his left hand rests on one of the pothead's shoes: from time to time he tugs gently and absently at the shoelaces. Koberling resents Max's unprejudiced trust in this pothead. What an idiot, Koberling thinks. Max, this guy's what I'd call an idiot.

Anna sits cross-legged in a wicker chair, staring at Koberling, and lapses into childhood recollections. "Something once happened with you, Koberling. Some peculiar business, I can't remember what exactly. I only know that you and my father were sitting at the kitchen table late into the night. Hey, Koberling, do you remember?"

Koberling makes no attempt to help her. He could haul out that business about the slap. He could tell her that as a child, during those summers in the country, she really was brown as a hazelnut. He could flatter her and remind her of all the silly children's jokes she used to tell, which her clown father proudly wrote down in an orange-colored notebook. He could tell her that she used to be skinny and wiry, that she would disappear in the morning, taking the bridge across the river, into the woods, and not come back till evening, scratched all over, her legs covered with ticks. He could say, "Your clown of a father left you alone. He allowed you to do whatever you wanted, so you'd simply disappear for the entire day. You weren't really there, not for any of us, and presumably that's your big childhood trauma today."

But he doesn't feel like it. She's of no interest to him. Her clown father no longer is of any interest to him. He would like to sit here, in silence, undisturbed. Koberling lights another cigarette and realizes that he has been grinding his teeth all this time. Constance comes walking up the gravel path, a bounce in her step, dreadfully relaxed. Too late, Koberling thinks, too late my dear, now they're here and they won't be leaving soon.

Constance recognizes Anna immediately. She smiles a beaming and convincing smile, claps her hands softly, and briefly holds them up to her face. She laughs, and plants her hands on her hips. Koberling is disgusted. He can anticipate what she's about to say: "Anna! Skinny little Anna, and at least fifteen years older now. I can't believe it's really you sitting here!" Anna beams, looking embarrassed. She introduces the pothead, then looks over at

Koberling, shy. Koberling suddenly pushes back his chair and flees into the kitchen. Skinny little Anna. What nonsense. He takes olives, cheese, salami, out of the refrigerator. Cut the bread, uncork the wine, the same as back then, the same as always. Now we'll eat supper, Koberling thinks. Now we'll eat, now we'll do something, even if it's only eating the goddamn food.

Darkness comes early because it's almost fall. Under the plum trees at the back of the garden the light is already gray; the Oder will be pink and light blue by now. Koberling thinks it's taken him forty-seven years to find out that the wheat fields and the lakes and rivers become light again just before night falls. He needed this house to find that out. Maybe Max, and Constance, too. If things were normal, the child would already be asleep, snoring softly, his cheeks red. He himself would be sitting on the veranda with Constance, reading or not talking. At some point he would sit down at his computer and type two or three sentences of dialogue for one of the screenplays that he writes for a living. Two or three short and strange sentences, as on every other evening. The light of the desk lamp would be green, because green is calming. The moths would tumble against the window screen, and he would find it both good and shitty living like this.

Now, though, the pothead is standing on Napoleon Hill rolling himself a joint. What a jerk. His absurd Zippo lighter flares up, and Koberling can smell the sickly-sweet hashish. He thinks of Rose Martenstein. Rose Martenstein, who came to a carnival party dressed as the Queen of the Night and collapsed, unconscious, on the kitchen floor after eating a hashish cookie: a doll in black satin. Sure, he had smoked hashish, too. With Anna's clown father, for one. They'd be sitting in the garden, smoking one joint after another, and Anna's clown father would shout, "Swazi grass!" and "Off to Swaziland!" till Koberling fell off his chair, laughing. Anna would be sleeping in her room under the mosquito net, talking in her sleep, and Koberling didn't know that twelve years later his own round-headed child Max would be born. How should he have known? How could he have? Back then he didn't even want to acknowledge Anna.

The pothead on top of Napoleon Hill turns around and motions to Koberling with his joint. Koberling gestures back an exaggerated refusal, and the pothead shrugs and ambles down off the hill. The glowing end of his joint disappears between the plum trees, and Koberling lingers irresolutely near the kitchen door. Constance and Anna are still sitting on the veranda, Max on Constance's lap, his thumb in his mouth. The child hasn't said a word to Koberling in the last four hours. He has clung to Anna or the pothead by turns, behaving as though he'd never seen a human being other than his mother and Koberling. Koberling thinks that's wrong. Max should be hiding behind him, should be asking him whether these guests are okay or not.

Anna talks about Poland. Max stares at her and from time to time breathes deeply, in and out. "I can't understand why you still haven't been there when it's so close. They have storks there the way Berlin has pigeons. The Poles were mowing the fields, and sixty or seventy storks were walking in the furrows behind the tractors, looking for insects. And you wouldn't believe what ice-cream eaters the Poles are. *Lody* and *lody*, wherever you look, they're constantly eating ice-cream."

Max takes his thumb out of his mouth and says very clearly, "Ice-cream." Koberling feels tenderness creeping up his back. What a weird conversation. And the child picks out the one word he knows—ice-cream.

Anna talks, gestures with her hands, is constantly tucking her hair behind her ears. "Constance. How are you doing here?"

Constance's voice, very deep and a little husky. Doing well. It's lonely. Koberling doesn't want a lot of visitors, a retreat after all those years in the city, a summer retreat; anyway in the fall it's back to Berlin. Long days. Hot days. Koberling spending a lot of time at his desk—a lie—and she herself going on walks through the Oderbruch, the Oder marshes, a most beautiful piece of nature. Good for the child, too. Children belong in the country. Max is happy; she is, too. And Koberling? He has trouble with being happy, but still . . .

Constance's hand, always arranging things. Constance, the perpetual organizer. Four, five sentences, a life forged from a single casting, one stroke of the pen and no more questions. It's that simple. In the shadows by the kitchen door Koberling closes his eyes and opens them again. Anna has stopped talking. Now, in the total darkness, a sudden indignant croaking of frogs. A brief moment. Anna lights a cigarette and says, "Yes," begins again to tell her Poland stories, the ice-cream stories, her voice sounding somewhat remote, disconcerted. In the dark

Koberling senses Constance's smile. He is surprised at how calmly she sits there listening to Anna's stories. In fact he is surprised at the interest she's showing in these guests, the obvious pleasure she takes in their visit. It doesn't matter who comes, Koberling thinks. It just doesn't matter. Anyone could be sitting here and she'd listen the same way, eagerly, glad to have a break from me for a while. It's because we've been here by ourselves the entire summer. But that's what we had agreed to do. We wanted to be by ourselves. I wanted to be alone.

Koberling goes back into the kitchen, turns out the light, and sits down on Max's little daybed by the window. The contours in the garden have become sharper. Anna's red dress is dark, appears black. Koberling looks at her and feels nothing. She is young, has her father's clown face, everything round, round eyes, round mouth. A gap between her teeth that's going to make her look common ten years from now. Brown hair, very brown skin.

She's probably taking classes at the university, Koberling thinks. Journalism, and a foreign language. The pothead probably tends bar in some trendy hangout and apart from that squanders his days. In the summertime they load their friends into old cars, drive to the

Brandenburg lakes, drink wine until they pass out, and are convinced that the things that happen to them don't happen to anyone else. Idiotic. All of it idiotic. He rubs his eyes and feels tired. The days when he used to ask everyone, "What do you think?" and "What do you do?" are over. Koberling can't imagine that he ever asked these questions. Disgusting, almost embarrassing, recollections of sitting around in bars all night, of swapping ideals, the destruction of illusions, carefully tended common interests. Hypocrisy, all of it, Koberling thinks. Anna's clown father was always just waiting for me to stop speaking so that he could begin with his utopias, his crazy head-in-the-clouds realities. And the same with me. I argued with him, I just wanted to outtalk him, when actually we both should have kept our mouths shut.

Max slides off Constance's lap, walks across the veranda, and stands at the kitchen door. "Why d'you sit there in the dark?" His voice is a little hoarse.

"Darkness is the friend of thieves," Koberling says. "Come on. Time for bed, time for the sand dragon and all that stuff." He stands and lifts Max up: the child smells of summer and country-road dirt. "Promise me," Koberling feels like saying to him, "promise me that . . ." But he doesn't say it.

"Are you two going to bed?" Constance asks from the veranda, her wicker chair creaking as she gets up.

"Yes," Koberling replies, hurrying to the stairs, "we're going to bed." In his arms Max is already asleep. Anna calls out, "Good night, Koberling!"

When he wakes up the next morning she is standing at the foot of his bed, smiling, her head cocked like a bird's. Glittering sunlight streams in through the window, and a fly bumps against the glass. Koberling squints in the bright light and gropes under the covers for Constance, who is no longer lying beside him. No dreams, he thinks with relief. I didn't dream, not about her clown father nor about the past, not about smoking grass nor about sex.

Anna is shaking the bedstead so hard it sets her hair flying. "Koberling! You sleepyhead! It's already noon, the others all drove into town, and breakfast is ready. You're supposed to get up and show me the Oderbruch!"

"Says who?" Koberling asks. He is suddenly furious, sleep in his eyes and a bad taste in his mouth. That Anna should have dared to come in here, bursting into the intimacy of his bedroom like a child. She probably sneaked through the house first, looking into chests and drawers with her naive curiosity. Koberling sits up and pulls the covers over his chest. "Out," he says, "get out now. I want to get up by myself. I want to be left in peace."

Anna lets go of the bedstead, still smiling, and walks towards the door. "I'll be in the garden, in case you want to know." Koberling doesn't want to know and doesn't answer. He waits until he hears her footsteps downstairs in the kitchen and closes his eyes again. Lying there. Just lying there, in a state of exhaustion, on a seesaw between waking and dreaming. He has never felt refreshed and rested in the morning, after eight hours of sleep. Always exhausted. Before, at night in his one-room apartment, Berlin and winter, he used to go to sleep dreading all the days, months, years that still awaited him. Time. Time that had to be filled up, conquered, annihilated. Then Constance came. A shared two-room apartment, Berlin and winter. In his memory always winter, warmth under the quilt, the commitment to Constance that was connected with a feeling of capitulation. Constance, behind whom Koberling hid and never emerged. Refuge and acquiescence. They used to fall asleep next to each other, saying, "Fly slowly." Time retreated, his dread crouched in the farthest recess of his mind. Then finally Lunow, this house, the breathing of the child, time completely dissolving. And then again the dread—even greater than ever before—some nights when a car drove by and projected the circling shadow of the venetian blinds onto the ceiling of their room. Perhaps because of that his exhaustion. Because sleep has to overcome dread, always.

Finished, Koberling thinks. Finished and done. It can't be that two little people from Berlin can walk in here and get me all confused. Confused about what? He gets up and opens the window. The fly moves out into the open in a straight line and is gone. Outside, the sky, a vast blue vault, and a newly woven spider web trembling in the window frame.

In the kitchen there's coffee on the table and an egg tucked into its woolen cozy. Constance has left him a note. "Dear Koberling, went shopping with Max and Tom, back sometime in the afternoon, why don't you show Anna the Oderbruch, hugs and kisses."

Show Anna the Oderbruch. An imposition. Koberling looks at the little beelike squiggle that Max has put under Constance's large flowing script and places his hand on his stomach. He rolls the egg undecidedly across the wooden tabletop, pours coffee into a mug, and sits down on the veranda. Anna, barefoot, is in the orchard picking raspberries. The midday heat is oppressive and close, and Koberling already longs for the evening. The coffee is lukewarm and bitter, leaving a furry taste on his tongue. Koberling pours it over the veranda railing into the flower bed and says softly, "For Janis."

Anna looks at him and picks up the berry bowl, then comes up onto the veranda. "What did you say?"

Koberling doesn't look up but gazes into his empty coffee cup and says, "For Janis. Your father always used to say that, long ago, when he poured leftover wine into the garden, 'For Janis, for Janis Joplin.' "

"Yes," Anna says simply.

Koberling doesn't dare look up. Suddenly he feels terribly embarrassed about something. He stares at Anna's feet, at her dirty little toes.

She hides her left foot behind the right. Says, "I thought I'd stay behind. Otherwise you would have waked up and found us all gone."

Koberling looks up now, and acts preoccupied. Anna tilts her head and smiles at him, unsure. "Wasn't it okay to wake you?"

What can you say to that? Nothing. And Anna doesn't seem to expect an answer. She sits down next to him, lights a cigarette, and inhales deeply. "Tom likes it here. I do too. It's so peaceful, and, besides, we're having an Indian summer."

Koberling makes a sound that could be interpreted as agreement or disapproval. Anna stares at him sideways. Koberling becomes restless and turns the empty cup in his hands; he can feel that Anna is slowly tensing up.

"Do you want to show me the Oderbruch or not? I mean, do you feel like going for a walk with me, or would you rather keep on sitting here?" With the last words her voice gets louder, almost stern.

Cry a little, Koberling thinks. Cry a little because you don't know how to deal with me, and also because I remind you of the time I slapped you. He too lights a cigarette, then gets up, and says, "Yes, well. We can go for a little walk if you want."

As Koberling closes the garden gate behind him he feels he's in unsafe territory. The house, the garden, the veranda, and above all Napoleon Hill are no longer protecting him. His back against the wall. Anna stands in the road, shifting from one foot to the other and looking almost the way she did long ago, like the child from back then, across the bridge over the river, into the woods, and away.

Koberling marches off resolutely, Anna hurries along

beside him, dust whirling up between their feet. The country road becomes narrower. At the foot of the hills it turns into a small path that winds upward, through fruit trees, up into the green. Koberling, hands in his pockets, stares straight ahead. He feels a tension in his back and is already grinding his teeth again. Anna aside. Even without Anna, he has never liked the walks into the Oderbruch. Constance does. Ever since Lunow has been there for her, Constance walks off every afternoon with a happy face and comes back with an even happier face. "The hills, Koberling. Sometimes I think it's the hills. I find them calming."

Koberling finds the hills disturbing. For him it's all too beautiful, too enchanted, a Tarkovsky landscape, almost sinister. Once last summer he went into the Oderbruch by himself. In a tree on one of the more distant hills—he could already see the Oder—hung a piece of meat. A big piece of meat, almost the size of a man—a cow or a pig—skinned, bloody, putrid, flies buzzing around it. Koberling, panting up the hill, ready to see the Oder, to savor it, stopped and felt his heart lurch. The meat hung from one of the upper branches, the rope by which it was attached creaking and twisting. It looked like a vision, like a nightmare image, a monstrous and incomprehensible message, and Koberling turned, ran back down the hill, and screamed. Later, Constance, sitting in the wicker chair on the veranda and smelling of violets, laughed and said, "Don't be silly, Koberling. You must have been dreaming."

The next day, when they went to the Oderbruch together, the piece of meat had disappeared. Nothing there any more. No rope, no flies, no message. They never talked about it again.

Anna kicks little pebbles, smiling again, and whistles through the gap in her teeth. "You don't want to talk, do you?"

"No," Koberling says, "I don't want to talk." Says to himself, Talk about what? and peers through the fruit trees, straining to see. There is no vision. Nothing that he would see but Anna would not.

"That's all right," Anna says. "I don't want to talk, either. A lot of times I don't." Koberling looks at her in ironic surprise, but she ignores him.

The last stalks of wheat still stand tall along the edge of the path. The trees have yellow edges, and a flock of birds forms a triangle in the sky. In the distance the Oder gleams, a blue ribbon perforated by green river islands.

The air above the fields shimmers. Anna is breathing heavily. She twists her hair into a bun at the back of her neck.

Koberling remembers the beginning of a poem, "On the far side of the Oder, where the plains so wide," or something like that, one of the countless poems he used to recite to Anna's clown father on those lunatic walks, at night, on the moors. "Listen to this one, and this one," a helpless recital, a gush of words. Koberling walks along behind Anna, and his inability to describe, to express why the words sound so heart-wrenching—"On the far side of the Oder, where the plains so wide"—leave him breathless. "I understand," Anna's father had said, again and again. "I do understand." But he couldn't have understood, because Koberling himself didn't comprehend anything. He would like to grab Anna by the hair now, to shake her and slap her for the years of self-deception, just for the years themselves. He wants to slap her again, to repeat himself. The Oder is dazzling, and the flat fields flow together into a green sea. Koberling calls her name and hears his voice, but as if coming from a great distance. Anna turns around, her red dress swinging into a wave. Koberling closes his eyes and thinks he is falling.

"Koberling? Are you all right?"

"Yes," Koberling says. "Everything's fine. I just want to go back now."

Shortly before they reach Lunow—they can already see the country road; behind the bend the house is about to appear—Anna touches his arm. Koberling takes a deep breath. The Oder is behind him, behind the hills, the distant unease already nearly forgotten. This will be the last time he surrenders to it. Koberling quickens his pace. He would like to walk fast, to run, perhaps even to sing. An enormous relief spreads through him.

Anna stops and says, "Koberling, I'd really like to know what there was between my father and you. I mean, I'd like to know why you no longer see each other, why you lost touch."

Koberling also stops and looks at her. She is smiling and looks hurt. "There's no reason. There's no story there." Koberling is surprised that he has even answered her. "We had a few really good years together, then we saw each other less and less frequently, and at some point not at all anymore. Maybe it was because he had women I didn't like. And you got older, later on he spent a lot of time taking care of you. There were minor arguments we didn't clear up, some disagreements. We lived different lives, I think. That's all. No tragedies, nothing decisive."

Anna turns around and takes the path through the field down to the road. She walks very quickly. Koberling follows her, wanting to call out, "Life isn't a play, Anna!" He doesn't know whether she can still hear him. She's running.

That evening Koberling is sitting on the veranda with Constance. Anna has gone back to the Oderbruch with the pothead. They had eaten supper together, and Koberling had three glasses of wine. He feels the alcohol in his knees and in his stomach. A cloud of mosquitoes hangs over the plum trees, and Constance is blowing smoke rings into space.

"I hope that Max will never do that. I'm not just hoping he won't, I simply won't have it," Koberling says, not looking at Constance but at the plum trees, out into the darkness of the garden.

"What?" says Constance sleepily. "What . . . will never do what?"

"What Anna did here," says Koberling and hears a note of spite in his voice that he can't avoid. "What she did by turning up here unexpectedly and under false pretenses. When Max grows up I don't want him to turn up at Anna's father's place with some floozy on his arm and say, 'Hey, clown father!'" Koberling raises his voice and mimics Anna. "'Hey, clown father, can we stay with you for a couple of days? Only a couple of days, nothing special, just to hang out, and at some point or other you can tell me why you stopped being friends with my father back then.'"

Constance laughs and forms a big smoke ring with her lips. It glides away and dissolves. "You're crazy, Koberling. Max doesn't even know Anna's father. And you probably aren't going to tell him anything either. And by the time Max grows up, Anna's father may no longer be around."

Next morning Constance and Max are singing along with the radio in the kitchen. Koberling is awakened up by their voices, which mix with that of the radio announcer. The sun is streaming through the window. No Anna in the room, no dreams during the night.

A summer day, Koberling thinks, picture perfect. He rumbles down the stairs, and pulls open the kitchen door. Max is sitting at the table, his mouth smeared with egg, looking blissful. Constance stands at the stove, her face a dark shadow against the sunlight. She doesn't look up, sings along with the radio, says, "Good morning, Koberling."

"Yes," Koberling says, looking out into the garden, to the veranda, toward Napoleon Hill. Then says much too quickly, "Where are they?"

The kettle begins to whistle. Constance turns off the gas and says, "They left already. Anna wanted to go to some lake or other before it got really hot."

Koberling goes over to the radio and turns it off. It becomes quiet in the kitchen. "What? I don't understand. Why did they leave so soon?"

Constance pours hot water into the coffee filter, her expression strained. "They didn't want to wake you again, Koberling. To abuse your hospitality. They left their address in Berlin and said they'd be delighted if we visited them in the fall."

Koberling stares at Max. Max stares back and lets his egg spoon sink slowly onto the table. Koberling feels an ache in his stomach, like a tremendous insult. He opens the door to the veranda and pokes his left hand through a spider web between the doorposts. Indian summer. He says, "By the time we go back to Berlin in the fall I'm sure they won't be together anymore," the one pathetic putdown he can think of. Constance doesn't answer.

Summerhouse, Later

I T W A S winter when Stein found the house. He called
me, some time in early December, and said, "Hello,"
then nothing. I didn't say anything either. He said, "This
is Stein." "I know," I said. He said, "So, how's it going?" I
said, "Why are you calling?" He said, "I've found it." Not
quite comprehending, I asked him, "What did you find?"
and he answered irritably, "The house! I found the house."

The house. Now I remembered. Stein and his talk
about *the* house, away from Berlin, a country house, a
manor house, an estate house, linden trees in front, chest-
nuts at the back, sky above, a Brandenburg lake, at least
two and a half acres of land; maps spread out, marked up,
driving around the area for weeks, searching. Then whenever he came back he looked weird, and the others said,
"What's he talking about? Nothing's ever going to come

of this." I forgot all about it when I didn't see Stein anymore. Just as I forgot about him.

As always when Stein randomly surfaced and I couldn't think of much to say, I automatically lit a cigarette. Hesitantly I said, "Stein? Did you buy it?" "Yes!" he shouted and dropped the phone. I had never heard him shout before. And then he was back on the line, still yelling; "You *have* to see it, it's incredible, it's great, it's fantastic!" I didn't ask why I, of all people, had to see it. I kept listening, even though for a long time he said nothing more.

"What are you doing right now?" he finally asked. It came out downright obscene, and his voice trembled slightly. "Nothing," I said. "I'm just sitting around reading the paper." "I'll pick you up. In ten minutes," Stein said, and hung up.

Five minutes later he was here. He didn't take his thumb off the bell even after I had opened the door. I said, "Stein, that's annoying. Stop ringing." What I actually wanted to say was, Stein, it's freezing outside, I don't feel like driving out there with you, just leave. Stein stopped ringing the bell, cocked his head, seemed on the verge of saying something, said nothing. I got dressed. We drove off. His cab smelled of cigarettes. I rolled down the window and turned my face toward the cold air.

❦

At that time my relationship with Stein, which is how the others referred to it, had already been over for two years. It hadn't lasted long and consisted mainly of trips we took together in his cab. His cab was where I'd met him. He'd driven me to a party, and on the Autobahn he had pushed a Trans Am tape into the tape player; when we arrived I told him the party must be somewhere else, and we drove on; and at some point he switched off the meter. He came home with me, set his plastic bags down in my hall, and stayed for three weeks. Stein had never had an apartment of his own, but moved around the city with these plastic bags, sleeping wherever he ended up, here and there, and when he couldn't find anything he slept in his cab. He wasn't what you'd consider a homeless person. He was clean, well dressed, never seedy, and he had money because he was working. He simply didn't have his own apartment. Maybe he didn't want one.

During the three weeks Stein lived at my place we drove around the city in his cab. The first time we went down Frankfurter Allee, all the way to the end and back again, listening to Massive Attack and smoking. We drove up and down Frankfurter Allee for probably an hour, until Stein said, "Do you get it?"

My head was completely empty. I felt hollow and strangely detached. The street ahead of us was broad and wet from the rain, the wipers moved across the windshield, back and forth. The Stalin-era buildings on both sides of the street were huge and strange and beautiful; the city was no longer the city I knew, but was autarkical and deserted. Stein said, "Like a giant prehistoric animal." I said I understood; I had stopped thinking.

After that we spent a lot of time driving around in his cab. For every route Stein had a different kind of music: Ween for the smaller country roads, David Bowie for downtown Berlin, Bach for the avenues, Trans Am only for the Autobahn. We almost always took the Autobahn. When the first snow fell, Stein would get out of the car at every rest stop, run to the snow-covered field next to it and perform slow and precise tae kwon do movements until, laughing and furious, I called out for him to come back. I wanted to get going, I was cold.

At some point, though, I'd had enough. I packed his three plastic bags and said it was time for him to find a new place to stay. He thanked me and left. He moved in with

Christiane, who lived on the floor below me, then with Anna, then Henrietta, then Falk, then with the others. He screwed them all, unavoidably; he was pretty good-looking. Fassbinder would have been delighted with him. Stein was always there with us, and yet, somehow, he wasn't. He didn't really belong, but for one reason or another he stayed. He posed as a model in Falk's studio, set up the cable system for Anna's concerts, listened to Heinze's readings at the Red Salon. He applauded when we applauded at plays, drank when we drank, did drugs when we did. He was there at our parties, and in the summer he came along when we drove out to the shabby, lopsided little country houses that everyone owned before long, and on whose rotting fences someone had scrawled *"Berliner raus!"* And now and then one of us would take him to bed, and now and then one of us watched.

Not me. I didn't repeat. Frankly, it wasn't my kind of thing. Nor could I remember what it was like—what sex with Stein had been like, that is.

We hung out with him, there in the gardens and houses of people we really had nothing to do with. Workers had lived there, small farmers, and amateur gardeners who hated us and whom we despised. We avoided the locals; just thinking about them ruined everything for us. It didn't feel right. We robbed them of their feeling of exclusivity, and we disfigured the villages, the fields, even the sky; it was in the way we strode around with our Easy Rider gait, flicked our joint butts into the flower beds in their front yards, the way we nudged each other self-importantly. But regardless, we wanted to be there. Inside the houses we tore down wallpaper, removed rubber and plastic; Stein did that, actually. We sat in the backyard, drank wine, gazed idiotically at *Tree Clump Circled by Swarm of Gnats,* and talked about Castorf and Heiner Müller and Wawerzinek's latest flop at the Volksbühne Theater. When Stein had finished he sat down with us. He had nothing to say. We did LSD, and so did Stein. Toddi staggered into the evening light, jabbering on, something about "blue" every time he touched anything. Stein smiled with exaggerated cheerfulness and said nothing. He simply couldn't get the hang of our sophisticated, neurasthenic, fucked-up expressions, even though he tried; for the most part he watched us as though we were actors performing on a stage. One time I was alone with him, I think it was in the garden of Heinze's house in Lunow, the others had set off for the sunset, on speed. Stein was putting away glasses, ashtrays, bottles, and chairs. Soon he was done and there was nothing left to remind us of the others. "Do you want some wine?" he asked. "Yes," I said." We drank and smoked in silence, and he smiled every time our eyes met. And that was it.

Now, as I sat next to Stein in the cab, on Frankfurter Allee heading toward Prenzlau in the afternoon traffic, I thought, And that was it. The day was hazy and cold, the air full of dust, tired drivers next to us, ogling and stupid, giving us the finger. I smoked a cigarette and wondered why I was the one who had to be sitting next to Stein now. Why, of all people, he had called me—was it because, somehow, I had been a beginning for him? Because he couldn't get a hold of Anna or Christiane or Toddi? Because none of them would have gone with him? And why was I driving out there with him? I couldn't come close to an answer. I threw the cigarette butt out the window, ignoring the comments of the driver next to us; it was awfully cold in the cab. "Is something wrong with the heater, Stein?" Stein didn't answer. It was the first time the two of us had been alone in his car since back then. Indulgently I said, "Stein, what kind of house is this? What did you pay for it?" Absentmindedly, Stein glanced into the rearview mirror, ran red lights, changed lanes incessantly, drew on his cigarette until the glowing tip reached his lips. He said, "Eighty thousand. I paid eighty thousand marks for it. It's beautiful. I took one look and I knew—this is it." He had red spots on his face and kept pounding on the horn with the flat of his hand as he pulled ahead of a bus that had the right of way. I said, "Where did you get eighty thousand marks?" He glanced at me briefly and answered, "You're asking the wrong questions." I decided not to say any more.

We left Berlin. Stein drove off the Autobahn and onto a country road. It began to snow. I felt tired, as I always do riding in cars. I stared at the windshield wipers, into the whirling snow coming toward us in concentric circles, and thought about driving like this with Stein two years ago, about the odd euphoria, the indifference, the strangeness. He was driving more calmly, glancing at me every now and then. I asked, "Doesn't the tape deck work anymore?"

He smiled, said, "Oh sure. I didn't know . . . whether you'd still like it." I rolled my eyes. "Of course I do," and pushed the Callas tape—the one on which Stein had recorded the same Donizetti aria twenty times in succession—into the tape deck. He laughed. "You still remember." Callas sang, her voice rising and falling, and Stein sped up and slowed down. I had to laugh, too, and I briefly touched his cheek. His skin was unusually bristly. I wondered, What's usual? Stein said, "See." I saw that he immediately regretted it.

After Angermünde he turned off the main road, stopping in front of the driveway of a low building dating back to the sixties; he braked so hard that I hit my head against the windshield. Disappointed and alarmed I asked, "Is this it?" This seemed to please Stein. With exaggerated movements he slid over the icy concrete toward a woman in a house dress who had just emerged from the front door. A pale, puny child clung to the house dress. I rolled down the car window, heard him call out with jovial warmth, "Mrs. Andersson!"—I had always hated the way he dealt with these kinds of people—saw how he offered her his hand and how she didn't take it but dropped a huge bunch of keys into it. "No water when it's below freezing," she said.

"Supply line's broken. But they're gonna turn the power on next week." The child hanging on to her house dress began to cry. "That's okay," Stein said, slid back to the car, stopping at my rolled-down window to rotate his pelvis elegantly and obscenely. He said, "Come on baby, let the good times roll." I said, "Stein, stop that." I felt myself blushing. The child let go of the woman's dress and took an amazed step toward us.

"They used to live in it," Stein said as he restarted the engine; he went in reverse back onto the road. The snow was falling more heavily now. I turned around and saw the woman and the child standing in the illuminated rectangle of the doorway until the house disappeared behind a curve. "They're mad because they had to get out a year ago. I wasn't the one who kicked them out, though, it was the owner from Dortmund. I only bought it. As far as I'm concerned they could have stayed on." "But they're disgusting," I said, not comprehending, and Stein said, "What's disgusting really?" and threw the bunch of keys into my lap. I counted the keys; there were twenty-three, small ones and very large ones, all old and with beautifully curved handles. I sang under my breath, "The key to the stable, the key to the attic, the one for the gate, for the barn, for the parlor, for the dairy, mailbox, cellar, garden gate," and suddenly—without really wanting to—I understood Stein, his enthusiasm, his anticipation, his excitement. I said, "It's nice that we're going there together, Stein." He refused to look at me and said, "In any case, from the veranda you can see the sun setting behind the church tower. We'll be there soon. After Angermünde comes Canitz, and Canitz is where the house is."

Canitz was worse than Lunow, worse than Templin, worse than Schönwalde. Gray, cowering houses on both sides of the twisted country road, many windows boarded up, no store, no bakery, no inn. The snow flurries were getting heavier. "A lot of snow here, Stein," I said, and he replied, "Of course," as though he had bought the snow along with the house. When the village church appeared on the left side of the street, beautiful and red with a round bell tower, Stein started to make an odd humming sound, like a fly bumping against a closed window in the summer. He drove into a small cross street, brought the car to a stop, simultaneously taking his hands off the steering wheel with an emphatic gesture, and said, "That's it."

I looked out of the car window and thought, That's it for another five minutes, maybe. The house looked as though at any moment it might cave in, suddenly and soundlessly. I got out of the car and shut its door with care as if every tremor might be too much. Stein and I walked toward the house cautiously, on tiptoe. The house was a ship. It sat at the edge of that Canitz village street like a proud vessel beached in times long gone. It was a large, two-story country manor house of red brick; its skeletonized gable roof had two wooden horse's heads, one at each end. Most of the windows had lost their glass panes, the crooked veranda was held together only by a dense tangle of ivy, and cracks as wide as a thumb ran through the brickwork. The house was beautiful. It was *the* house. And it was a ruin.

The gate from which Stein was now trying to remove a "For Sale" sign collapsed with a small plaintive sound. We climbed over it, I paused, startled by the expression on Stein's face. I saw him disappear behind the ivy on the veranda. Moments later a window frame fell off the house, Stein's excited face appeared amid the jagged shards of glass in one of the panes, lit up by the light from a kerosene lamp.

"Stein!" I called up. "Get out of there! It's going to collapse!"

"Come in!" he yelled back. "It's *my house*!"

I briefly asked myself how that answer was supposed to be reassuring, then stumbled over garbage bags and trash onto the veranda. Its boards groaned, and any light was immediately swallowed by the ivy; in disgust I pushed the vines aside, then Stein's ice-cold hand pulled me into the hall. I grabbed it. I grabbed for his hand; suddenly I didn't want to lose his touch again, and especially not the glow of his puny little kerosene lamp. Stein was humming. I followed him.

He pushed all the shutters out into the garden. We could see the last of the daylight through the red splinters of glass in the doors. The bunch of keys that felt so heavy in my jacket pocket was totally unnecessary, as all the doors either stood open or were no longer there at all. Stein held up the lamp, pointed, described, stood breathlessly before me, wanted to say something, said nothing, pulled me along. He stroked the banisters and door handles, tapped on walls, picked at the wallpaper and marveled at the dusty plaster underneath. He said, "You see?" and "Feel this" and "How do you like that?" I didn't even have to answer; he was talking to himself. He knelt on the kitchen floor and wiped the filth off the tiles, muttering; I clung to him all this time, yet I no longer existed. On the walls, somebody had scrawled "I shot the moon tonight. I was here, Mattis. No risk, no fun." I said, "I shot the moon tonight," Stein turned toward me, suddenly confused, and said, "What?" I said, "Nothing." He grabbed my arm and pushed me along in front of him, kicking open the back door that led out into the garden and dragging me down a few stairs. "Here."

I said, "What do you mean—here?"

"Well, everything!" said Stein. I had never seen him so insolent. "A Brandenburg lake, chestnut trees in the yard, one and a half acres of land, you can plant your god-damn weed here, and mushrooms and hemp and shit. Plenty of room, you understand? Plenty of room. I'll build you a salon here, and a billiard room, and a smoking room, and separate rooms for everyone and a big table in back of the house for your shitty meals and crap, and then you can get up and walk over to the Oder and snort your coke there until you fry your brain." He twisted my head roughly in the direction of the garden and the land be-yond. It was too dark, and I could scarcely make out a thing, I began to shiver.

I said, "Stein. Please. Stop."

He stopped. Fell silent. We looked at each other; we were breathing hard and almost in the same rhythm. Slowly he put his hand on my face. I flinched; he said, "All right. All right, all right. Okay."

I stood still. I didn't understand any of this, though remotely I did understand something, but it was still too far away. I was exhausted. I thought of the others and felt a surge of anger that they had left me here alone, that no one else was here to protect me from Stein, not Christiane, nor Anna, nor Heinze. Stein shuffled his feet and said, "I'm sorry."

I said, "It's okay. Don't worry about it."

He took my hand; his was warm now, and soft; he said, "So: the sun behind the church tower."

On the veranda he brushed the snow off the steps and gestured for me to sit down. I did. I felt incredibly cold. I took the lit cigarette he held out to me. I smoked, staring at the church tower, behind which the sun had already set. I had the vaguely guilty feeling that I should be saying something forward-looking, something optimistic. I felt confused. I said, "In the summer, I'd pull the ivy off the veranda. Otherwise we can't see anything if we want to sit there and drink wine."

Stein said, "Will do."

I was sure he hadn't been listening at all. Sitting next to me he seemed tired. He looked out at the cold, empty, snowy street; I thought of last summer, of that hour in

Heinze's garden in Lunow, I wished Stein would look at me one more time the way he had looked at me then, and I hated myself for thinking it. I said, "Stein, would you please tell me something? Could you please explain something to me?"

Stein flicked his cigarette into the snow and looked at me. "What should I tell you? This, here, is one possibility, one of many. You can go with it, or you can forget it. I can go with it, or I can forget it and go somewhere else. We could do it together, or pretend that we never knew each other. It doesn't matter. I only wanted to show it to you, that's all."

I said, "You paid eighty thousand marks to show me one possibility, one of many? Did I understand that correctly? Stein? What's the point?"

Stein didn't react. He leaned forward and looked intently out into the street. I followed his gaze; the light was dim and the last rays reflected by the snow made it hard to see. Someone was standing on the other side of the street. I squinted and sat up. The figure was about fifteen feet away; then it turned and walked into the shadows between two houses. A garden gate banged. I was convinced I had recognized the child from Angermünde, the pale, dumb child that had clung to the woman's house dress.

Stein got up and said, "Let's go."

I said, "Stein—the kid. From Angermünde. Why is it hanging out, here on the street, watching us?"

I knew he wouldn't answer. He held the car door open for me, I paused in front of him, waiting for something, for a touch, a gesture. I thought, But *you* always wanted to be with us.

Stein said coolly, "Thanks for coming with me."

I got into the car.

I no longer remember what kind of music we listened to on the way back. In the weeks that followed I saw Stein only rarely. The lakes froze over, we bought ice skates, and at night we roamed through the woods and out over the ice, carrying torches. We listened to Paolo Conte on Heinze's boom box, swallowed Ecstasy, and read aloud the best parts from Bret Easton Ellis's *American Psycho*. Falk kissed Anna, and Anna kissed me, and I kissed Christiane. Sometimes Stein was there, too. He kissed Henrietta, and whenever he did I looked away. We avoided each other. He hadn't told anybody that he had now finally bought the house, nor did he tell them that he had driven out there with me. I didn't either. I didn't really think much about the house, but sometimes, when we threw our ice skates and torches into the trunk of his cab before driving back to the city I saw roofing paper, wallpaper, and paint.

In February Toddi fell through the ice on Lake Griebnitz. Heinze was skating wildly across the ice, holding up his torch and shouting, "This is so much fun, we're having such a great time, I can't believe it!" He was completely trashed, and Toddi was skating along behind him. We called out, "Say 'Blue,' Toddi! Say it!" and then there was a crack, and Toddi disappeared.

We stood still. Heinze, his mouth open, came back around in a terrific loop, the ice hummed, wax dripped hissing from our torches. Falk took off on his skates, tripping, Anna tore off her scarf, Christiane stupidly covered her face with her hands and whimpered. Falk crept along on his belly, Heinze was nowhere to be seen. Falk yelled for Toddi, and Toddi yelled back. Anna cast out her scarf; Henrietta clung to Falk's feet. I came to a stop. Stein also stopped. I took the lit cigarette he held out to me. He said, "Blue," I said, "Cold," and then we began to laugh. We laughed, doubling over, and lay down on the ice, and tears ran down our cheeks; we laughed and couldn't stop, not even when they brought Toddi back, wet and shivering, and Henrietta said, "Are you crazy or something?"

In March Stein disappeared. He didn't turn up for Heinze's thirtieth birthday, or for Christiane's premiere or Anna's concert. He was gone, and when Henrietta, pathetically discreet, asked where he was, they just shrugged. I didn't shrug, but I didn't say anything either. A week later his first postcard arrived. It was a photo of the village church in Canitz, and on the back it said:

> *The roof is waterproof. The child is blowing its nose, doesn't speak, is always here. The sun never lets you down, I smoke when it's setting. I've planted something you can eat. I'll cut the ivy when you come. Remember, you still have the keys.*

After that the postcards came regularly. I waited for them; when they failed to come, I was disappointed. They always had photos of the church and always four or five sentences like little riddles, sometimes nice, sometimes incomprehensible. Stein often wrote "when you come." He didn't write "Come." I decided to wait for "Come," and then I would go. In May there was no card, instead a letter. I looked at Stein's clumsy, large handwriting on the envelope, crawled back into bed with Falk, and tore open the envelope. Falk was still asleep and snoring. Inside there was a newspaper clipping from the *Angermünder Anzeiger*. Stein had scribbled the date on the back. I pushed Falk's sleep-warmed body aside, unfolded the article, and read:

REGIONAL NEWS

On Friday night the former manor house in Canitz burned down to its foundation. The owner, a Berliner who bought the eighteenth-century house six months ago and restored it, has been reported missing since the fire. The cause of the fire has not yet been established. So far the police have not ruled out arson.

I read it three times. Falk moved. I stared at the article, then at Stein's handwriting on the envelope, then back at the clipping. The postmark said "Stralsund." Falk woke up, looked at me apathetically for a short moment, then reached for my wrist and, with malicious shrewdness, asked: "What's that?"

I pulled my hand away, climbed out of bed, and said, "Nothing."

I went to the kitchen and for ten minutes stood mindlessly in front of the stove. Above the stove a clock ticked. I ran into the back room, pulled out the desk drawer, and added the envelope to the other cards and the big ring of keys. "Later," I thought.

The author would like to thank the Autorenwerkstatt Prosa (Prose Writers' Workshop) of the Literarische Colloquium Berlin, the Kulturfond, the Akademie der Künste, the Alfred Döblin Haus in Wewelsfleth, and especially Katja Lange-Müller, Burkhard Spinnen, and Monika Maron for their support during her work on this book.

Author photograph by Susanne Schleyer

ABOUT THE AUTHOR

Judith Hermann lives in Berlin, where she works as a freelance writer. *Summerhouse, Later* is her first book.